Elaine Ellis

POSTMAN'S Knock

'The grass is always greener' turned out to be an artist's impression, not real life at all.

Elaine Ellis

POSTMAN'S Knock

~~~

'The grass is always greener' turned out to be an
artist's impression, not real life at all.

ROMAUNCE
Cirencester
~~~

1A The Wool Market Dyer Street Cirencester Gloucestershire GL7 2PR
An imprint of Memoirs Publishing www.mereobooks.com

Postman's Knock: 978-1-86151-836-1

Published in Great Britain by Romaunce Books,
an imprint of Memoirs Publishing Ltd.

A CIP catalogue record for this book is available from the British Library.

The address for Memoirs Publishing Group Limited can be found at
www.memoirspublishing.com

Cover design and artwork - Ray Lipscombe

The Memoirs Publishing Group Ltd Reg. No. 7834348

The Memoirs Publishing Group supports both The Forest Stewardship Council® (FSC®) and the PEFC® leading international forest-certification organisations. Our books carrying both the FSC label and the PEFC® and are printed on FSC®-certified paper. FSC® is the only forest-certification scheme supported by the leading environmental organisations including Greenpeace. Our paper procurement policy can be found at www.memoirspublishing.com/environment

Typeset in 11/17pt Century Schoolbook
by Wiltshire Associates Publisher Services Ltd. Printed and bound in Great Britain
by Printondemand-Worldwide, Peterborough PE2 6XD

CHARACTER LIST

Charlotte Whitfield	25, Married to James. Talented businesswoman.
James Whitfield	28, Husband to Charlotte, Computer programmer.
Libby Gordon	25, Best friend of Charlotte. Lady of leisure.
Bruce Gordon	28, Husband to Libby. University friend of James.
Georgina Harvey	27, Sister of Charlotte. Schoolteacher.
Tom Harvey	30, Husband to Georgina. Air traffic controller.
Alan Peters	55, Charlotte and Georgina's father. ATC retired.
India Peters	Charlotte's mother. Deceased aged 50, 3 years ago.

CHAPTER 1

"Dear Charlotte,

This is going to be the hardest letter I have ever had to write.

I was hoping our friendship through school and university would survive into our dotage, but I have my doubts and I won't blame you if you feel unable to forgive me."

Charlotte read on, stopping just long enough to take a deep breath.

"Because of our friendship I've decided to be 'up front' and to deceive you no longer."

The letter Charlotte was reading arrived in the post after James had gone off to the office. She was still sitting at the breakfast table in her dressing gown, sipping her coffee. In anticipation of bad news, she put her coffee cup down and read on.

"James and I have fallen in love. We tried to stop our feelings, for your sake, but they were just too strong."

Charlotte stopped reading and looked at the seat James had recently vacated, across the breakfast table. She wondered how he could have acted so normal, eating his breakfast, kissing her goodbye, wishing her a good day and telling her he'd see her later. He could have got an Emmy for his performance. He should have got a smack, she thought. Tears were pouring down her cheeks. She wanted to have her shower, get dressed, and go and give Libby a smack too. But instead, she mustered the courage to read on with difficulty. She realised she was shaking uncontrollably.

"I don't know where we can go from here, but we are all adults. I'm sure we could still be friends, eventually, but at least over the next few months' civility and decorum will be a reflection of our upbringing. Hopefully we can rise above name calling, it's futile and will end in upsetting you."

That was the final straw; Charlotte stopped crying and was now angry.

"The patronising, husband-stealing bitch from hell!" She shouted. Well, that had already proved Libby wrong. Calling her a name had made Charlotte feel much better actually.

She looked at the final sentence in disbelief...

"Lots of love, as always, Libby X."

Charlotte decided to wait to see if James came home. She wasn't going to talk to him on the phone, or by email. She also didn't want to alert him or Libby to the fact she had received the letter that morning, until she had worked out what to do next. It also occurred to her that Libby's husband Bruce may not have been told yet. Poor Bruce, she suddenly thought. He was such a gentle man. The repercussions of that morning would affect too many people for her to go off screaming 'affair' before she had thoroughly thought it through.

She needed a plan. After showering and dressing, she decided to go and talk everything through with her trusted confidante, her sister Georgina. Since their mother had died a few years previously, the sisters had got closer, if that was possible. There was only eighteen months between them, Georgina being the eldest. Their father had always called them George and Charlie, making people think he had two boys. It amused him. Their mother had insisted on calling them both by their full Christian names. The girls had enjoyed a wonderful life with their parents, growing up with security and love that helped them through the tough times life had to throw at them.

As Charlotte arrived at her sister's house, she was glad to see her car in the driveway, with the added bonus of her father's car on the road.

Georgina opened the front door just as Charlotte was about to ring the bell. She had heard her sister's car.

"Charlie, darling, whatever is the matter?" Charlotte thought she had been so brave, but on seeing her sister the full force of the last hour had hit her. Tears flowed and her shoulders raised and fell without any authority from her brain. Georgina ushered her sister into her kitchen and just cuddled her until the sobbing subsided. Charlotte managed to get the now crumpled letter out of her handbag and gave it to Georgina. Charlotte watched her sister as the contents of the letter sunk in.

"Oh my goodness. The utter bitch. I never liked her. She was always up her own arse." For the first time that morning Charlotte had a smile on her face. Her sister was the only one who could make her laugh during a crisis. "I say James is very welcome to her. He'll only last five minutes before he comes snivelling back with his tail between his legs. She'll eat him alive. And that is when you say, 'bugger off you bastard. I've always been too good for you'." She smiled at her sister.

It was having the desired effect. Charlotte was looking stronger and more resolved than when she arrived. No longer the victim. She was in control. That was until her dad came in from the garden for a cup of coffee, having been helping Georgina's husband, Tom, build a shed.

"Hello poppet, didn't know you were here." He went over to give her a cuddle and the tears involuntarily started again. Georgina put the kettle on and handed her dad the letter. He read it with an unfamiliar frown on his brow. "Well, what a little strumpet, I've never liked her. Too stuck-up; looks like a horse in my opinion." Charlotte realised that crying wasn't possible when you needed to laugh. They were all laughing as Tom came in. He was about to give Charlotte a cuddle when Georgina thrust the letter into his hands. Tom read it and looked extremely puzzled.

"What's the matter? Can't you read her writing?" Georgina passed him a coffee.

"No, it's not that. This woman has just admitted to having an affair with your sister's husband, so I just don't understand why you were all laughing about it when I came in. Have I missed something?" Poor Tom. He was so lovely. He wouldn't cheat on Georgina; she wouldn't let him!

Having been brought up to date on the name calling of Elizabeth Gordon, Tom joined in the family discussion of what Charlotte should do next.

They all agreed that Charlotte should carry on as if nothing had happened, throwing Libby and James into a panic.

After lunch and when all plans had been discussed, Charlotte went home to resume her wifely chores and prepare dinner as usual. She wasn't even sure if James would be back, or if Libby may or may not accompany him for moral support, but she was determined that normal service will be resumed and she would then be ahead of the other two.

She had to admit to being a little nervous as she spoke to her sister for the umpteenth time.

"Just follow the plan. Don't give anything away with your body language. Are you sure you don't want me to hide in your wardrobe in case you need me?" Charlotte smiled. Just knowing her whole family was there for her gave her a massive confidence boost. She was ready to face James. He was due home any moment. Would he come? Bang on time she heard his car in the driveway. She went into the kitchen.

"Hello darling, had a busy day?" she shouted from the kitchen. She could hear James rifling through the post in the letter rack on the hall table. Charlotte had left a few bills unopened to show him that the post had arrived that day, but no sign of the dreaded letter. James popped his head round the kitchen door.

"Usual, you?" Charlotte handed him a glass of red wine as was normal. He felt reassured that Charlotte knew nothing.

"Usual. Dinner in half an hour, if you want a shower first." James nodded, took his wine and disappeared upstairs, glancing once more at the letter rack. Breathing a sigh of relief, he knew he had one more evening of calm to enjoy Charlotte's cooking for the last time. Was he having second thoughts? Was he being bulldozed? He couldn't think straight. A shower and the wine would help.

As soon as Charlotte heard the shower she went upstairs to their bedroom and found his phone on the bed.

Georgina had told her to make sure that James knew Libby had spilled the beans first. The only way of knowing would be to get into his phone and check his emails or text messages. Text messages were easier so she'd check those first.

Charlotte felt very uncomfortable. She had never invaded James' privacy before. She'd never had cause to. George had insisted that this was war, in which case the niceties of life don't count. She needed to know what the enemy was up to.

James was in the en suite, so Charlotte had to be quick. If he suddenly walked out wet, he'd catch her. She touched his screen and got prompted for the code. Had he changed it? No, he wasn't very good at clandestine, cloak and dagger, having affairs sort of thing, obviously. She put in the code that was the same as the house alarm, all his credit and debit card pin numbers, and also the small wall safe they had in their wardrobe. That reminded her of the first thing she had to do on his vacating the marital home, change all the codes. The water was still in full flow, so she clicked on the message bubble, and checked through the names. L Darling was the latest. Well, unless it was another character from the *Blackadder* series, she thought not, then that must be Libby darling. Instinct told her Libby had probably put that into James' phone herself. He was never that romantic. She wanted to throw up. She touched L Darling on the screen. There must have been around ten messages from that day; she didn't have time to count. She randomly read one from the middle.

"Any news yet?" Sent from L Darling at 11.03.

James had answered, *"No, I'll let you know if I hear from her."* Within the hour, three more had been posted, all in the same vein. *"I take it you haven't heard anything?"* James was getting annoyed. Charlotte could tell the tone of his voice by his curt wording. *"I still haven't heard from her, not in the last 5 minutes since I last told you anyway."* She wasn't sure how much longer she could risk reading, but had to read the last one.

"You'll have to act normally and hope it arrives tomorrow. I hope it hasn't got lost in the post James. I can't possibly put up with this for much longer. My nerves won't take anymore." Poor Libby, thought Charlotte, with a grin on her face. Her curiosity had certainly strengthened her resolve. The shower suddenly went quiet. She came out of the messages onto the home screen and turned off the phone and quietly went downstairs.

She was feeling so strong. Georgina had said that if there was any proof he knew about the letter, it meant he was too chicken to face her in person. He would be more relaxed after his shower. He'd think Charlotte would have exploded as he got in the front door if she had read Libby's letter, or at least have changed the locks. Charlotte had convinced him she knew nothing. He was walking straight into her trap. She grinned inwardly, she was sure of a BAFTA by the end of the evening.

"Smells good." He looked at Charlotte over the other side of the kitchen and smiled. If he could read her thoughts he'd be shocked. The language she was using was not very lady-like. On the other hand, she could read him like a book. He was having doubts. She surprised herself by her own resolve. He was now defunct as a husband; soiled goods, defiled by another woman.

They sat and ate in companionable silence, only broken by the odd compliment for the meal, a normal evening of late. Funny thing was, it was only then that Charlotte realised she had lost him a while ago. Gone was the old banter over dinner. The funny happenings of the day relived by them both. When did all that stop, she wondered? Probably around the time he started enjoying Libby's company. Perhaps he was worried he'd let something slip, so thought best to play safe and not talk except about the here and now, the meal, the mundane. Her laid-back, relaxed attitude was hiding an anger build-up she was trying to control; but timing was everything.

She had been busy that afternoon, after she left Georgina's. She had been to the bank and taken half the funds out of their joint account. She paid them into her personal account for safekeeping. She needed to keep cash flowing for bills, so couldn't risk James suddenly panicking and emptying it all. After all it was her hard work and brains that had got the business going in the first place.

She had used Georgina, and her inheritance trust from their mother, to put an idea into action. She had been to university and as a postgraduate got an MA in Marketing Communications. Charlotte's idea came to her one evening while they were trailing through the Yellow Pages for a takeaway. She started a site which relied on takeaway restaurants paying a fee to be on the website, and supplying their menus. She went around the country organising clients in person and online selling her idea, until she had enough interest to start. James then designed the website, having attained a software engineering degree. Simple ideas are always the best. Basically, you go online to the website, homepigout.co.uk, choosing which takeaway food you want; entering your postcode, which gives you the nearest restaurant and their menu should be displayed for you to choose and pay for online and it will be delivered to your door within the hour. Now it was worth a fortune.

The meal finished, having eaten his favourite chocolate torte, Charlotte was playing a wicked game; she wanted him to leave on a high! Libby had never cooked for their dinner parties; they had always had caterers in. Would that be his last home-cooked meal until Christmas with the in-laws? She tried to keep a straight face.

James sat back in his chair, licking the chocolate from his lips.

"That was delicious, thank you." He was sated, relaxed and it was almost like he had forgotten what the next day would bring.

Charlotte waited until he was ensconced in front of the television, coffee by his side. She went upstairs to add a few more items to the small case she had packed earlier and hidden. There were some items he had been wearing and some were in the bathroom he needed for his shower, but now they could be packed. She had to leave it until the last minute so as not to arouse his suspicions.

She carried it downstairs and put it into the lobby, between the front door and the outer door.

On cue, having texted Georgina that dinner was over, the doorbell rang. She opened the door and handed the driver the suitcase.

"James. It's for you." James got off the settee and went to the door, looking anxious. Please God, don't let it be Libby, he thought, or worse still Bruce to punch his lights out. He looked out of the door to see a man walking down towards the front gate, suitcase in hand.

"Who is it?" Charlotte handed him his jacket, phone and pointed to his shoes in the lobby.

"It's your lift." James looked at her puzzled. "To your new life. I hope you will be very happy. My solicitors will be in touch with you in the morning. Goodbye James." She had managed to manoeuvre him into the lobby where his shoes were waiting for him, before he realised what was happening and before he was able to reply, she shut the inner door and deadlocked it.

She ran upstairs, before he left the lobby. From her bedroom window, she watched him walk down the path towards the taxi. He was talking animatedly on his mobile phone. He instinctively turned and looked up to where Charlotte was standing. He could see her silhouette through the voiles, but luckily her tears weren't visible. She saw him mouth the word 'sorry'. She almost turned to run down the stairs and call him back in. He then ruined the moment by mouthing the words 'I love you' just before he turned to get into the taxi. She wasn't a fool. Words were cheap, actions spoke louder. If his last few words had meant anything to him he would not be leaving in that taxi but thumping on the front door asking for forgiveness. How could he have 'carried on' behind her back, with her ex-best friend and then have the nerve to say those words?

No, she thought, it wasn't love he felt. It was security, comfort, even stability. He had a lovely home, an attentive wife, a job and a good income. The irony was that they had worked hard to attain all those things, and he was now walking away from them. "What an idiot." She said aloud. But was she talking about James or herself?

Within minutes Georgina and Tom were at her back door. Tom poured Charlotte a glass of wine while the sisters discussed what to do next.

As they were deliberating, the front door bell rang. Tom told the girls to stay put, just in case it was James back, or worse still James and Libby. Tom went to open it, ready to close it back into James' face, but it wasn't James, it was Bruce. He looked awful.

It appeared that James was on the phone to Libby and Bruce overheard the commotion and asked Libby "What was going on with poor old James?"

"Charlotte has chucked him out. He's having an affair." Bruce obviously asked Libby if she knew who with. She answered with a smirk, "Me!"

"Well, you could have knocked me down with a feather. I hadn't a clue." He'd walked straight past James and got into the still-running taxi and decided to come and check on Charlotte. Bruce was brought up to speed with events of the last day.

"I am so sorry Charlotte." Bruce was such a lovely man. His world had just collapsed and he was worried about Charlotte, apologising for his wife. Having found out that Bruce's family all lived in Scotland, Tom told him he was to stay with them until he knew what he was going to do next. He had left in a daze and hadn't even taken a toothbrush.

Tom played golf with Bruce and James every Saturday, so they were quite close. It was a shock to them both.

"What about FFF. It was our turn this Friday." Charlotte was referring to their dinner party club. The six of them had had dinner in each other's houses on the first Friday of every month. It was called the Fun First Friday Club, FFF for short. It had started with just Charlotte and James and Georgina and Tom. Then one day Charlotte decided to play matchmaker for her old friend Libby and James had said he'd bring his work buddy Bruce along, as he was alone in a 'foreign' country having left his home in Scotland. That was just under two years ago.

James and Libby had ruined so much with their affair. It was going to have a massive knock on effect with them all.

That night Bruce went back with Tom. Georgina, who'd had the forethought to pack a small overnight bag stayed with Charlotte. She had a feeling that her sister was putting on a brave face, but the full force of what had happened would probably hit her in the early hours, when the defences are at their lowest ebb. She was right and stayed holding her sister until she went still and her breathing pattern finally slowed.

CHAPTER 2

~

The next morning, being all cried out, Charlotte felt so much stronger. She made an appointment with her solicitor, Jeremy, just before lunch. Jeremy had been her parents' solicitor and her mother's executor and was unreservedly trusted by Charlotte and the rest of her family.

She busied herself all morning getting accounts together and other important paperwork. She was going to make sure that Elizabeth Gordon did not end up with the profits from all Charlotte's hard work. She had used her mother's money and her heart and soul into getting the business started, working into the early hours when most of the takeaway restaurants were doing the bulk of their trade, catching the owners as they cashed-up. She enjoyed every minute of it, even if it had been hard. She was not going to fail her sister who had allowed her to use her share too in the venture. Georgina always had faith in her clever sister.

Charlotte was not going to disappoint her.

Tom had taken Bruce off to the golf course to help him plan a strategy. Poor Bruce worked for Libby's father in his computer programming business. Not only was that going to be awkward, but the further he got from that family the better.

At her solicitors, the secretary showed her into Jeremy's office.

He went through the legal formalities of firstly selling the company. As the 'A' shareholder she had all the voting rights and benefit value of the company on selling. James had 'B' shares, which meant he had no voting rights (which meant Charlotte could sell without asking him) and would only get dividends that would reflect the value of the sale.

As the money used to finance the company had been an inheritance trust in Charlotte and Georgina's name from their mother's family, James had no claim at all.

Jeremy told her that she would come out of the sale a very wealthy woman. Charlotte was pleased. That had been her aim all along. She wanted to make enough so Georgina could leave her job of teaching. Her heart had gone out of it. The curriculum had changed in the short time she'd been teaching GCSE Literature, so much so that instead of the children wanting to read a good Shakespearian play, Dickens, or a beautiful poem by Wordsworth or Keats, they were reading books like Terry Pratchett's *Discworld*. Times had changed, but for the literary scholar, not, unfortunately, for the best. For a young woman, she was old-fashioned when it came to her passion for books, just like her mother.

The house had been bought and lived in before James had even met Charlotte, so he would have to fight very hard for a share of the house. Apart from that, Jeremy told Charlotte that if James had a good solicitor, he might manage to get maintenance from her. Before she left she had arranged to put the company on the market, which Jeremy would do for her, and also to start divorce proceedings. She would never be able to trust James again, and didn't want to waste any time in getting free from him.

She left the solicitors with a strong will and a focus. She would need to start a new company up as soon as she'd thought of one. She sat in the coffee shop opposite the solicitors, drinking a double espresso, jotting down notes of things to do, under the title 'Life Begins Today'. The enormity of her situation suddenly hit her. Financially she knew she was fine, but emotionally she suddenly felt lonely. She knew she had all her family around her whenever she needed them, but nothing can beat the last snuggles of the evening before dropping off to sleep. She suddenly had a very silly thought; perhaps she'd buy a puppy. She hadn't been able to have any pets, because of James' asthma. As she finished her coffee she thought, "what a difference a day makes". A strange feeling took over all her senses and she rushed to the Ladies.

Georgina told her later that it was probably delayed shock. Hardly surprising and she had tried to carry on as if nothing had happened, not giving in to the urge to shut herself away and ignore the outside cruel world as a victim.

Far from it, financially she had no problems, but her brain needed stimulating, she needed another project to keep her sane. She had gone back to Georgina's and was sitting with Bruce in the garden. She asked him if he'd had time to think of his future. He said he'd already handed in his notice to Brian Bennett-Palmer, Elizabeth's father, that morning. He was now on gardening leave until the end of the day's trading! It had made him feel better. He had taken control of his life. Fat lot of good it had done him though. He now had nowhere to live and no job. He'd thought of popping into town and asking where he could get hold of some copies of the *Big Issue*. At least he'd have enough money to buy a Big Mac. He was laughing at himself. Charlotte liked the way Bruce didn't take himself too seriously.

"Well Bruce if you are on the market I would like to snap you up. I have an idea for a new business venture which I would like you to help me with, if you have no other ties at the moment." Bruce felt the adrenalin sear through his body. He wanted a challenge and Charlotte had thrown down the gauntlet. He agreed to join her in her venture, without even hearing what it entailed. Her ideas were brilliant and that was all he needed to know. They shook hands on it.

Bruce was waiting for Tom to get home so they could get a few holes in before the light failed. Tom had been at work since six o'clock in the morning and would be knocking off early. He was an air traffic control officer at the local airport in Christchurch. He had been Charlotte and Georgina's father Alan's star pupils at the ATC College, based at Bournemouth airport. So much so that Alan used his influence with the CAA to get Tom his first position locally. His first Christmas as a fully-fledged Controller meant that his shifts left him no time to get to see his family in Cornwall. So Alan had taken him home for a Christmas meal with his family. Romance blossomed with Alan's eldest daughter and the rest, as they say, is history.

Over the next few weeks Charlotte with the help of Bruce and her sister's knowledge of the literary industry, had set up an idea in principal. It was then up to Charlotte to sell it to the general public, her forte. It kept them busy. They were all actually enjoying themselves, until a text or email brought Bruce or Charlotte back to reality with an unpleasant jolt.

During the first few weeks Bruce had heard nothing from Libby apart from the initial first text telling him to pick up the five bin liners with his stuff in from the garage between the hours of 1 pm and 2 pm on the first Tuesday after he'd left. She announced that she'd make arrangements for him to pick up larger items, here she mentioned one 'the grotesque grandfather clock' he had brought down from Scotland having been left it in his grandmother's will. Bruce loved the chimes on the hour every hour, as it reminded him of his childhood and many happy holidays spent with his grandparents in Forfar near Perth, where they had a smallholding with chickens and pullets as well as fruit and vegetables. He remembered strawberry picking as a child with his cousins, when his Nanna Kathy would give them punnets to fill. They ate so many it took a long time to fill them. Their Nanna Kathy never minded, there were far more than she could sell in a season, and if the children were full of strawberries it didn't cost so much to feed them at teatime. Then there was the jam she'd made from them warm and sweet spread on homemade bread fresh from the range. At moments like that, Bruce wished he'd married a Scottish lass. He felt very home sick. He confided all this to Charlotte.

"Oh, Bruce. Please do not think all English women are like Libby. She is definitely a one off!" Charlotte passed Bruce a glass of wine. They had been brainstorming for hours and deserved a treat. She carried on; "No true English girl would take her best friend's husband from under her nose." Her wine glass was empty and was just about to pour another when she had an overwhelming desire to throw up. She ran out of the kitchen and left Bruce looking very worried. She was back in no time and wondered what Bruce was doing as she could only see his back. As he turned he had a plate of sandwiches made up.

"Don't say no, you haven't eaten since I've been here and that's probably why you were queasy on one glass of wine." He put the plate in front of her and sat down to watch her eat them.

"Are you not having any?" She was touched by Bruce's concern, but still couldn't get used to eating alone.

"I've got a casserole in my slow cooker waiting for me. Don't look like that, I'm actually a domestic God." He did make her laugh, and that was probably the best medicine for them both. "You forget I did all the cooking for Libby. She found it difficult to hold a grater, for fear she'd break a nail!" They were both laughing again.

"Well I think they both deserve each other, James and Libby. James never cooked a thing. He wasn't worried about breaking a nail, his inertia maybe, but not a nail." Bruce watched Charlotte finish the last cheese sandwich and cleared her plate away.

"The more I think about it, the more I realise that they have both done us a favour. Better to find out their true colours before children had come along." Bruce said over his shoulder. He was by the back door. He didn't want to leave, but Charlotte needed rest. She looked peaky, he thought.

"You are right. At least we are young enough to start all over again with the right person." They both looked at each other and smiled. Bruce felt something he couldn't put his finger on. Charlotte got up and gave Bruce a kiss on the cheek. "See you in the morning. Night, Bruce." She shut the door and waved to him from the window. He was such a nice guy. Libby was a fool. Fancy dumping someone so kind and considerate and, she had to admit handsome, for a plonker like James. As her grandfather used to say 'There's nowt so queer as folk". She went off to bed taking Bruce's advice. An early night wouldn't do her any harm. Although lying in bed didn't automatically mean sleep. Her mind was always whirring and James still wasn't far from her thoughts.

Charlotte hadn't heard much from James at all. He'd have received the letter from the solicitors informing him of the impending divorce and sale of the business. She had expected him at least to ask for a timescale for both events, and what share of the business he was to have. But the lack of contact worried her. She couldn't help the flashbacks coming into her mind of his face looking up and the regret on it. Was he happy? Why did she care? She was cross with herself for even worrying. She had a new business to concentrate on and a new colleague to help her. Bruce was certainly a good worker, and also a good companion. With the thought of Bruce on her side and the business progressing on schedule she finally succumbed to slumber.

Charlotte, Bruce and Georgina finally got their website up and running, and it was a runaway success, just like the last one. Charlotte seemed to know exactly what people wanted and when they wanted it.

While Bruce had been setting up the website, Charlotte had been doing market research, targeting book clubs and drama groups for interest.

The site was to help novice writers of fiction/non-fiction, plays and poetry to get published. The idea was that people downloaded their work into the appropriate genre on the site. Then the general public could register membership, paying a small fee to read any of the books available. The membership was strictly monitored so admission was from genuine applicants with email addresses and follow up home addresses, which could be checked, and therefore it eliminated as much plagiarism as possible. Members could then read any item, and each time an item got a hit the writer got a royalty. There was a special membership for publishers, and if any find the next *Harry Potter*, with the permission of the author, their details will be passed onto the publisher and the publisher gave Charlotte's company commission. It was a win–win situation for writers, publishers and Charlotte's company. Bruce had managed to get a friend in to help with the security aspect of the website, and the finer points of online payments, while Charlotte managed to get a massive interest all over the country, with enquiries from as far as the United States and China. She'd have to organise translators, which was where Georgina was able to help. Luckily for Charlotte it was one of the hardest thing to get a manuscript published and there were a lot of frustrated writers out there.

Jeremy had left a message for Charlotte. It was fantastic

news, homepigout.co.uk had two major buyers, both trying to outbid the other, causing the price to go up beyond what Charlotte had thought it worth. She was able to pay Bruce a good salary on that basis, so he moved out of the bedsit he had been in since he left Libby and into a new rented flat overlooking the harbour in Poole. He loved it. It reminded him of his childhood when his summer holidays were spent with his Aunty Hennie and Uncle Ronnie in Arbroath, right on the harbour. He could still smell the Arbroath Smokies if he shut his eyes and loved listening to the rigging on the sail boats in the marina clanking rhythmically in the wind, outside his flat window. Life was becoming more bearable and he was looking to the future with anticipation and, he realised, contentment.

CHAPTER 3

Georgina had been keeping an eye on her sister for the past few weeks. Charlotte had told her the sickness had stopped but George could see she was still losing weight. Charlotte had joked that she had been too busy to eat, but George knew her sister was lying.

Charlotte only noticed something was wrong when she recently had to put a belt on her trousers. She knew she hadn't been sick for a few days so why would she be losing weight? She had put it down to a psychological problem and thought that as soon as she stopped thinking and worrying about James the symptoms would go away.

Luckily her sister was so worried she surprised Charlotte one evening with an impromptu visit. Charlotte was not expecting visitors and therefore had taken off her make-up and donned her favourite evening attire since James left, her trackies. George entered the house as she had started doing since James had moved out, by the back door.

"Cooee, it's only me." Charlotte got off the sofa and headed towards the kitchen where her sister had already put on the kettle for a cup of peppermint tea. "Hello old thing. Tom's playing squash with Bruce and I was bored." Charlotte knew that was just a ruse for her sister to check up on her. She was actually quite chuffed. "Cup of tea?" Charlotte shook her head. She had gone off tea and coffee lately. "Coffee?"

"No thank you. I've just had a cocoa." She pointed to a milk saucepan still on the hob. "I meant to put it in the dishwasher with the mug, but I forgot." She went over and grabbed the pan while George watched her.

"Charlie?" Charlotte closed the dishwasher door and looked up at her sister. "Don't get cross, but I've brought something for you." Charlotte wondered whether to be pleased or apprehensive. Looking at her sister's facial expression she decided on the latter. George went to the breakfast table where she had left her handbag and took out a Boots bag. "Take this to the bathroom and humour me." Charlotte looked into the bag and saw a pregnancy test kit.

"You are joking. I'm not pregnant. I've been stressed beyond endurance which is why I've been a little under the weather, but I can't be pregnant." Charlotte was trying to convince herself rather than her sister. Could she be pregnant? She tried to remember the last time James was 'in the mood', which was rarely until he left. "Oh my God." Charlotte suddenly remembered. "The only time in the last three months was when Chelsea beat Arsenal," she mimicked James' voice, "'keeping Chelsea on the top of the

Premiere League', apparently." Charlotte didn't follow the football but James explained it all to her that night, after he had 'celebrated' his team's win. She took the test kit into the downstairs toilet. When she had followed the instructions, she took it into the kitchen and handed it to her sister. She was too scared to look at the results herself. George watched the indicator window. Within no time two red lines appeared.

"Charlotte, you are pregnant! That explains all your health issues at the moment. Thank goodness for that. I was so worried. It's my own fault; I shouldn't look online for a diagnosis. It told me you had all manner of things, not at all nice." She realised that Charlotte was crying. Were they tears of joy? She couldn't tell. She rushed over and cuddled her sister tightly. "We'll be fine." She said reassuringly. "We'll get you to the doctors so you can have a scan to check the baby and see how far along you are. It says 3+ weeks, that could mean anything. Then we'll have so much fun buying clothes and baby equipment." Charlotte pushed her away gently.

"I'm not sure yet whether I want something so close to James." She took the test stick and threw it in the bin. George didn't know what to say. For the first time in ages she wished her mother were here to comfort and advise Charlotte in the way she used to.

Charlotte saw how worried her sister looked. "Hey, stop worrying. This baby is going to be loved very much." Charlotte broke into a huge grin. "Bugger James, I will have to tell him but he's not going to ruin this baby's life like he did mine. George?" Georgina looked at her sister. She really was finding it hard to keep up with Charlotte's mood swings, she knew she'd have to get used to them for a few more months anyway.

"Yes, I'm listening." Charlotte gave her sister a hug.

"I fancy marmite on toast with a banana squashed on top!" They both held each other laughing. "It's quite exciting when you think about it. If it's a girl I'd love to name her after Mummy. Would you mind?" George pulled away and held Charlotte at arms-length looking her straight in the eye.

"I think that would be a lovely idea. It is such a beautiful name it would be a shame not to." George felt quite emotional. Her hormones seemed to be mirroring her sister's.

"India, if it's a girl then. What should I name a boy?" She hoped it was a girl, but just in case she ought to think of a boy's name.

"You have months to think of a name. The important thing now is to check you and the baby are well. Phone the doctor for an appointment in the morning and let me know when it is. If you can get one after school I'll take you." Charlotte was pleased her sister was there for her. She didn't have a husband to help her now. Could she do this alone, she wondered? "Now off to bed with you. Would you like a bedtime story?" How could she think she had to do this alone with a sister like Georgina!

"OK, Mum! I'm off up now. Morpheus is waiting for me in my bed." George looked puzzled for a moment and then realised she was talking about the Greek God of dreams. They both hugged one more time and George left feeling a lot happier than when she had arrived. She was going to be an aunty, who'd have thought. Charlotte locked the door behind her sister and for the first time in a while was in bed and asleep before midnight.

Charlotte woke up feeling positive. She telephoned the doctor for an appointment and got one for the next evening. She sent Georgina a text with the time. The phone beeped back immediately.

"Good girl. I'll pick you up at 5.45 tomorrow. Love you both!! XXX"

Charlotte suddenly realised there were now two of them, her and the bump, not yet showing. She would have to tell James. She would keep it no matter what he said, but it was only right to inform him. It was also an excuse to go and see how he was. She decided to take the bull by the horns and visit him that evening, without warning. She hadn't seen James or Libby since the break-up of both their marriages. For some reason, she wanted to see James in his new surroundings, whether it was to make it real and therefore final, she didn't know. Or it could have been that she wanted to see how he was physically and mentally without him being warned first and able to prepare. She still didn't know why she was bothered. Perhaps she still loved him. But how could she after what he had done. Deep down she was blaming her best friend, ex best friend, Elizabeth Gordon. Elizabeth Gordon, nee Bennett-Palmer used to be her confidante. From early childhood in prep school, through boarding school and onto university Libby was always at Charlotte's side. Always asking for help with her homework, which Charlotte now realised she actually did for her. In fact, it was during their first year at university that Charlotte realised that Libby just couldn't hack it. She had been asking Charlotte to help her with an end of term presentation. Unfortunately, Charlotte had to decline as the workload was getting too much even for her. Libby flunked her first year and couldn't stand the humiliation of redoing the year so left. Her parents, who were a lot to blame for Libby being so spoilt, made her go to the local secretarial college so she at least had something to help her in adult life. Her mother was just as bad as Libby. She had insisted keeping her surname on marriage, Bennett, and also taking her husbands, Palmer, to make it double-barrelled. Charlotte was surprised that Libby hadn't done the same on her marriage to Bruce, Elizabeth Gordon-Bennett-Palmer. Actually, it did flow quite nicely! She'd just seen the funny side, Gordon-Bennett. That was probably the reason she hadn't triple-barrelled her name.

She was still going over her reasons for visiting James as she walked up to the front door. She rang the doorbell. James answered the door, in an apron. If Charlotte hadn't been so nervous she would have laughed. She'd never seen James in a pinny before. He looked tired. He was pleasantly surprised to see Charlotte at the door, but thought she looked awful. She'd lost too much weight. He went forward and kissed her on the cheek. Her skin was still as soft as he'd remembered it. He would have to use a trowel to feel Libby's skin.

"James." Libby snapped from inside the house. "Who's at the door?" James took a deep breath and sighed.

"Come in Charlie." He then shouted back to Libby. "It's Charlotte." He led Charlotte into the kitchen where Libby was sitting at the breakfast-bar, sipping a drink and reading a magazine. Charlotte couldn't help notice James rushing over to the hob and pulling a saucepan off, tutting. He stirred furiously and put the heat right down before replacing the saucepan back onto the hob.

"Charlotte, darling, how lovely to see you." Libby air-kissed her, but Charlotte had turned away before Libby had finished. Libby acted as if she hadn't noticed Charlotte's rudeness. "I was only saying to James the other evening that time has marched on and we must have you all over for an FFF dinner." Charlotte couldn't believe her ears. She looked at James who rolled his eyes to the ceiling out of direct sight of Libby. At least he was still on planet Earth, in the real world, thought Charlotte.

"I'll make this quick, James. I'm pregnant. I'm telling you as a matter of courtesy not for gain. I'm financially well-disposed and am capable of bringing the baby up alone. I want nothing from you. I just thought it fair to tell you out of respect as you are the father." Charlotte was glad to get that out. She had practised and practised to get it perfect and was able to deliver it without any interruption, her main intention. James had gone white as a sheet. Was she enjoying his discomfort? Actually, she had to admit she wasn't. Suddenly from behind her came a screech.

"You utter bitch!" Libby bawled. "So obviously a ruse to get James back. Well we are not falling for it. Tell her James. You little minx, did you really think you could fool us with such a sob story?" James watched Charlotte as she turned to leave. She was composed and was not going to satisfy Libby with a reply. "James tell her we would undoubtedly need a DNA test as soon as possible. I can't believe that Charlotte could stoop so low with such a juvenile ploy to get her man back."

"Libby, shut up." James was angry. He went into the hallway and ushered Charlotte into the lounge. He shouted over his shoulder to Libby. "Please keep an eye on the sauce while I talk civilly to Charlie." Both James and Charlotte heard a whinny from the kitchen and smiled. Charlotte suddenly thought her father was right when he likened her to a horse. "Please sit down for a moment Charlie. Can I get you a drink?" She shook her head. The sooner she got out of there the better; but she had to give James a chance to talk. "I can't believe it. I'm going to be a dad." He looked genuinely excited. It made Charlotte feel uncomfortable. She hadn't reckoned on James wanting the baby. "How far along are you?"

"I'll know more tomorrow when I've been to the doctor. I'm assuming it was on the night Chelsea beat Arsenal, so you do the maths." James smiled. Was that the memory of the match or the thought of beginning a new life? For the first time Charlotte found it difficult to read him. He'd changed in the last few months. She even noticed a few grey hairs. Poor James she thought. No, not poor James at all, what was she thinking? She took a deep breath, back to the job in hand.

"Obviously I will keep you informed as to its progress etcetera. I reiterate I do not want money from you. I will bring this baby up myself. I will, however, let you help chose the names and organise visitation for you once the baby is old enough to be away from me. Hopefully that would be at least six months as I plan to breastfeed." James nodded. He wouldn't have a clue what to do with nappies and bottles. He had his doubts as to whether Libby was maternal at all. No, Charlotte was being sensible. He agreed. "I would like to call the baby India if it is a girl, after my mother." James nodded again.

"Lovely idea. If it is a boy?" Charlotte sighed. She really didn't want a mini James in her life, but she'd still love it.

"I'll let you think about a boy's name. We have plenty of time. In the meantime, perhaps you can impress upon Libby that I'm not after financial gain, nor am I yearning for my ex-husband back." James looked like he'd been slapped in the face. Good, thought Charlotte, he deserved that. Sometimes words hurt more than actions. What Charlotte couldn't see in James' reaction was that his heart was actually breaking. He had got so excited about the baby he had almost put the two of them back together as a couple to bring up their child. Charlotte had thrown that thought out of the window in one verbal thrust.

Inwardly James blamed Libby, why they couldn't have kept their affair a secret, like they had for over a year, he didn't know. He'd lost everything, his job, his wife and now his child. Had it been worth it?

"Fricking Hell!" He heard Libby swear as she took the saucepan off the hob. There was a bang as it hit the sink and then he heard the tap running. He answered his own question with a resounding '*No*'.

Charlotte looked amused.

"Oh dear. I hope you have plenty of ketchup." James was actually smiling. He had missed Charlotte's sense of humour. "I'm sorry I've ruined your dinner James. I'll go now. I'll ring you when I've got more news as to the due date and so on." She reached up and kissed James on the cheek. He so wanted to take her into his arms.

"Yeow." Came another screech from the kitchen. "James!" Libby shouted.

"She's probably burnt her hand now." James ran to the kitchen. Before he reached the door, there was another wail.

"I've broken a nail now." Libby wailed; she was such a drama queen.

"Goodbye James." She wanted to add good luck, but thought it a little inappropriate.

He walked her to the front door and she left. Poor James, she thought. She couldn't remember him ever having to do anything domestic during their marriage.

Charlotte slept well that night, only to be disturbed by her phone beeping a message. She stretched over to see the name. It was from James. She checked the time, 06.45 a.m. The one morning she had slept passed 6.30 a.m., already she was cross!

"Hi Charlie, lovely to see you last night. Sorry about the pantomime! Managed to save enough so didn't starve! Hope to see you again soon. In the meantime, keep me up to date about our baby and if you need me to come with you to any appointment give me a bell. India Lima Yankee, James X."

Charlotte was well and truly awake having read the text. What planet was the man on, she thought? Firstly, the text sounded as if the past few weeks had never happened. Secondly, what part of 'I want nothing from you' did he not understand? Thirdly, was he honestly having a laugh? Tom had taught her and George the phonetic alphabet for fun and when she met James, full of romance and love, she had shared her knowledge with a simple India Lima Yankee after each of their messages to each other, meaning I Love

You. He had to be joking. After all the pain, heartache and hurt he had put so many people through, he had no right to put that at the end of her message. She was about to delete it, but then thought it would strengthen her and Bruce's resolve and so she kept it to show Bruce and George later.

Anger seemed to be a more positive approach than disappointment in James' attitude of playing with her emotions, especially in her condition. She was angry. To the point that in the shower she sung at the top of her voice, the only verse she could remember, of one of her favourite songs from *Kiss Me Kate* 'I Hate Men'. It just seemed so appropriate!

She felt revived, invigorated and nonchalant. They don't make songs like that nowadays, she thought. More's the pity! Her mother used to take her and her sister to shows all the time in their childhood. The thought of her mother seemed to give her more determination to put her best foot forward and get on with her day. Luckily she was meeting Bruce at nine o'clock so she had enough time to have breakfast and clear the things away before he arrived.

Bang on nine o'clock there was a knock on the kitchen door. Bruce knew Charlotte was still a little jittery about visitors and so in his best bellow he shouted through the door.

"Tis I, Bruce of The Glen." Charlotte heard him and laughed as she opened the door.

"You nutter. Come in and have a wee dram." They both laughed. "And what a bonnie morning it is too, to be sure." Charlotte wasn't very good at accents.

"You were doing so well until you lapsed into Irish!" He pecked her on the cheek as they had done before as friends and had continued now as colleagues.

"I have so much to tell you Bruce. Would you like a coffee?" Charlotte went to put the kettle on.

"It depends on how long it will take. I need to get some of these papers signed before midday so forget the coffee, just sit and tell." He patted the stool next to him.

Charlotte started with her visit to James and Libby's the previous evening. They both fell about laughing at Libby's dramatic scenes.

"I cannot believe how 'precious' she still is, in her parallel universe," Bruce admitted, shaking his head. "She needs a reality check, to be sure" He added in an Irish accent. Charlotte playfully thumped him.

"Libby has always thought of herself as a 'Lady' and therefore everyone else were her 'Servants'. I remember when we used to have play dates, Libby always played the Princess and I was made to play the rescuing Prince, or sometimes the scullery maid, or even the wolf, but never the Princess. Luckily, I've grown up, leaving such fairy tales behind, but unfortunately Libby is still in her make-believe world." Charlotte got her phone from the worktop by the kettle and opened the text message from that morning. She handed it to Bruce.

"Oh, my goodness, he's joined her in fantasy land." He wanted to keep

Charlotte cheerful. "They're coming to take him away ho ho, hee hee, to the funny farm where life is beautiful all the time, and he'll be happy to see those nice young men in their clean white coats..." His voice was getting quicker and squeakier to the point that he lost it for the moment. But it had paid off. Charlotte was laughing so hard that there was no need to carry on. Job done, he thought. Inside he was seething at James but that wasn't going to help Charlotte, so he'd keep that to himself to take out on a golf ball later. "I've had a thought." Bruce managed to get Charlotte to stop laughing and look at him. "Why don't we have a dinner party like the old days? We can invite Georgina and Tom and start a new group." He checked his watch. Charlotte misunderstood. She thought he was about to leave. Why would that disappoint her? She had to admit to herself that she did enjoy his company. His voice was like Sean Connery's, with a soft Scottish lilt, very soothing to the ears. "It's the third Friday in the month so we could call it the fun third Friday club, F.T.F. Club. Or we could call it the F.O.J.A.L. Club." Charlotte tried to work out what that stood for. "Feck off James and Libby club." Charlotte roared with laughter and Bruce joined her. It was quite funny, he thought, but it was actually funnier watching Charlotte's face contorted so much that she looked like a little squirrel. Bruce stopped himself. She was now his boss. There had to be some professionalism in their relationship. But he couldn't help wanting to protect her. He felt it was his role, his purpose, and his need. He was cut short in his thoughts.

"I'll ring Georgina and see if they are free. What a wonderful idea Bruce."

Charlotte was about to unlock her phone when Bruce stopped her.

"Shall we do it at my place? I'd love to cook. I'm getting withdrawal symptoms!" Charlotte smiled. She had to admit that Bruce was a good cook.

"That would be lovely, but shall we have the dinner here? You can still cook, but I'm worried you don't have much in your kitchen yet." Bruce nodded. That would be more practical. He had few chairs, less plates and his set of cutlery was very hit and miss.

"Ok, you're right. Can't ask everyone to bring a bottle, a chair and perhaps a plate and knife and fork. Oh, and glasses unless they want to drink wine from mugs. One condition to having it here though." Charlotte looked at him bemused. "You stay out of the kitchen for the duration. The whole point of me cooking is so you can relax and enjoy." Charlotte smiled. She didn't need to be told twice. By evening she tended to want to slum it in pjs and slippers.

"I fully agree to your terms. Now can I phone my sister?" Bruce nodded. While she was on the phone Bruce was writing out a shopping list on the back of an envelope he'd found unopened on the worktop addressed 'to the occupier', and a local estate agent's name emblazoned on the top. He was sure Charlotte did not need some wide boy upsetting her status quo at the moment. "That's settled, they will be round at 7.30 tonight. I'm looking forward to it already. Let's get those papers signed so you can tootle off to Waitrose!" Bruce hadn't seen her look so happy for a while. The evening was going to be therapeutic for them all.

Firstly, Charlotte had to get the doctor's appointment out of the way or her sister would nag her. At 5.45 pm George was outside peeping her horn. Charlotte had already calculated the age of the baby to between four or five months at least. She needed to get her pregnancy confirmed and onto her notes so a midwife can be appointed to her. She had been looking on the internet to see what was expected during antenatal care.

George stayed in the waiting room while her sister met

the doctor. He ushered her behind a screen where she lay down. He checked her blood pressure, her tummy and helped her up.

"Well I have to say you are one lucky lady." He was busy typing up her notes while she watched, bemused. Lucky to be pregnant? She wasn't sure what he meant. He turned round to her.

"You are at least eighteen weeks, probably a couple more. You are also one of the lucky ones not showing a bump yet. Quite normal with a first baby so don't worry." He turned back to his screen and typed a bit more. "So, I will book you into the antenatal clinic where you will meet your midwife and she can organise your care. You will need to have a scan very soon and blood tests. You will also need to take in a urine sample with you. The appointment will come through the post so don't worry, you are now in the system." He got up and put out his hand. Charlotte got up and shook it. "Congratulations, Mrs Whitfield."

"Thank you. Goodbye." She left feeling confident that whatever happens she was in good hands.

George dropped her back home and went to change and pick up Tom before she returned for dinner. Charlotte went in the kitchen door and was so happy to see the friendly face of the chef, albeit covered in flour.

"Hello, how did you get on?" Bruce pulled out a stool and made her sit and tell him all about her appointment. As she was telling him she realised that she was actually looking forward to being a mother.

CHAPTER 4

~

The food was superb and didn't include the threatened haggis! The company was relaxed and the conversation steered clear of divorces. It was just like old times, without Libby and James, who weren't even missed. In fact, both Charlotte and Bruce were more relaxed without the constant filthy looks they often received from their respective spouses for enjoying themselves. Georgina and Tom agreed, while Bruce and Charlotte cleared away and made the coffee, they were all having a good evening.

What they were all unaware of was a shadow outside the dining room patio doors. There was a small gap in the curtain where James could see in. He could hear the laughter and the glasses chinking, and looking in he saw a table of familiar faces enjoying an evening together. He wished he could ring the doorbell and join the company, but that would ruin everyone's evening.

He had come over to talk to Charlotte privately. It had taken him ages to pluck up the courage. Libby had gone to the sports club for a spinning class. James hadn't been too sure what that was, but didn't want to get into a conversation about it, he was just relieved he had the night off, even for a few hours. Which was why he was creeping behind the house he used to live in, listening to his friends having a nice evening. He was going to tell Charlotte that he was unhappy. The old proverb 'The grass is always greener' turned out to be an artist's impression, not real life at all. He actually thought Bruce owed him for giving him a lucky escape. Bruce, who was inside James' old dining room, enjoying the company without the looks, coughs and under the table prods, was actually thinking the same thing, true irony.

James drove home, he couldn't wait until everyone left, Libby would be home and he had no excuse for being out. Life was not working out the way he had wanted it to. He needed to get Charlotte alone and hope that her hormones while she was pregnant would make her more sympathetic towards his apologies.

He'd already thought of a few, 'can't believe what an idiot I've been,' and 'I've never stopped loving you,' and the ace up his sleeve, 'we need to think of our child, bringing it into this world with a mummy and a daddy, raising it together'. He had to get back soon. Didn't want to burn his bridges. He needed to keep Libby sweet until he had his old life back.

The new website, literallyworms.co.uk, was launched and took off immediately, much to Bruce and Charlotte's delight.

Champagne was drunk in abundance, Charlotte allowing herself a small bucks fizz, and an impromptu party prevailed.

Alan was so proud of his daughter, instead of dining out on her misery, she had knuckled down and started another business. Georgina was proud of her sister too. She was watching the computer screen and was amazed. The 'hits' were adding up by the minute and it was looking like it could overtake the last venture and be far more lucrative.

Charlotte didn't slow down. The site was more popular than her wildest dreams could have imagined. Bruce was worried she wasn't getting enough rest. The groundwork was in place, so it practically ran itself, but Charlotte was never happy resting on her laurels. She wanted to check all the emails and feedback herself. Getting Bruce to tweak up certain suggestions coming in from the public until it was perfect. With her appetite for marketing she was out looking for even more clients for her site. You could do so much electronically, she told Bruce, but nothing would replace the personal touch.

Two weeks after the launch, on a Friday, when Libby was at her spinning class, James was walking up to his old front door. He debated whether to walk straight in, find Charlotte, take her into his arms and carry her up the stairs in a warped version of *An Officer and a Gentleman*, but in reality the locks could be changed and Charlotte could be asleep and end up with a heart attack.

Charlotte was checking her emails, on the settee, drinking a mug of cocoa as she had gone off coffee and had chronic indigestion. She was just thinking about having an early night when the doorbell rang. She was in her pyjamas and winding down nicely, the warm milk having just started to settle her stomach. She wasn't happy having to get up to answer the door, especially as she wasn't expecting anyone. She glanced up to the right hand top corner of her laptop. It was nearly nine o'clock. A bit late for Jehovah's Witnesses, she thought. Perhaps it was Bruce, checking up on her. He'd been quite attentive, the busier they got. Trying to take some of the workload off her. Maybe there was a problem with the website that couldn't wait until morning. It couldn't be Georgina or Tom or her father, they'd have used their back-door keys. The doorbell rang again. Persistent, she thought. Maybe it was James, or Libby, or both. Whoever it was, they weren't going away. The caller was now knocking on the door. She grabbed her mobile phone, just in case she needed to call her sister quickly and got up. As she went towards the front door the doorbell rang again.

"Ok, I heard you the first time." she shouted. She opened the inner door to see James on the other side of the front door. She kept the outer door locked and talked to him through it.

"James, it's late. What do you want?" Charlotte was annoyed, he could tell by her sharpness.

"Please let me in. I *need* to talk to you." He sounded like a spoilt schoolboy, lingering on the word 'need'. Charlotte really wasn't in the mood for pleasantries. Her stomach had started feeling uncomfortable again.

"Say what you need to and go." His plan wouldn't work with a door between them. He needed at least to make eye contact.

"For old times' sake, let me in Charlie." Charlotte

thought he was really hamming it up. Normally she'd be quite amused, but not that evening. She needed the loo and wanted him to go.

"If you want to talk to me, choose a normal time of day and preferably somewhere other than my doorstep. Goodnight James." She shut the inner door and put out the downstairs lights. She was grateful her father had insisted she was to start locking the outer door. It had stayed unlocked when James had lived there. She listened intently resting her foot on the first step of the stairs, until she heard James' car drive off. She was gripping the bannister. She hadn't realised how scared she had been. James had never laid a hand on her, so why she felt threatened she didn't know. Must be her hormones, she thought. But then, did she know the real James? He certainly had been playing a part for a while. He wasn't the James she had fallen for and married. Or was he? Had he been acting all along? She needed to get up the stairs and into her bed. As she pulled herself up the stairs a gripping pain in her stomach bent her over in agony. She managed to crawl and pull her way up the stairs. At the top, she curled up into a ball and waited for the pain to subside. Her pyjama bottoms felt very cold. She reached down and realised they were soaking wet. She was gripped by another wave of pain and tried to crawl into her bedroom to get to her en suite. She made it to the threshold of her bedroom door and just rolled onto her back with her legs curled up onto her tummy. The pain subsided again. She was terrified. She took her phone from her pyjama top pocket put her thumb on the button then pressed the phone icon. For quickness she had put an A before Georgina's name so she would be on top of the list.

She touched it and the phone starting connecting.

"Hi Charlie, everything ok?" She was relieved to hear her sister's voice.

"Georgie, I think I'm losing the baby." She was crying.

"I'll be there in a mo. Hang on darling." Georgina shouted for Tom to get the car out of the garage as she grabbed Charlotte's back door key off their key rack.

By the time they got to Charlotte's she was in her shower room, passed out. Georgina called for an ambulance, only to be told there was one on the way. Charlotte must have managed to ring them before she passed out. Georgina saw Charlotte's pyjamas and wondered if she should try and clean her up a bit, but Tom told her to leave her still until the ambulance arrived. Any movement may make her bleed more. The paramedic arrived with an Emergency Medical Technician called Russell. He told Georgina and Tom to stay downstairs while John, the paramedic, assessed Charlotte. Eventually, as they carried the still unconscious patient down to the ambulance Russell told Tom which hospital they were taking her to and to make their own way there. Charlotte wasn't in any state to notice whether her sister had gone with her in the ambulance or not. Tom thought it a better idea that the Paramedic and EMT got on with what they were best at and Georgina stayed out of their way. Georgina, although being torn to protect her sister, knew Tom was right. They got into their car and followed the ambulance to the hospital, phoning her father on the way.

Charlotte could hear muffled voices.

"She's coming round. Dad, Dad, she's opening her eyes." Charlotte could hear movement. Someone was holding her hand. Then someone took her other hand. She could hear a woman calling her name.

"Charlie, it's ok. Tom and I are here with Dad. You're going to be fine. Wake up darling." Georgina wondered if she should get a nurse. "Tom, can you press the button? The nurse said to let her know when she woke up." Tom pressed for the nurse. Charlotte opened her eyes with a few blinks. She was trying to get used to the bright lights.

"Georgie, did I lose it?" Georgina was dreading the question, she hoped her sister would come to and just be glad she was fine. She nodded with tears in her eyes.

"Yes, my darling. But you are lucky to be here, so we count our blessings. You lost quite a bit of blood. But the doctor said you will be fine, as long as you rest." Charlotte felt her father's hand grip a little tighter and she turned to look at him. Poor Dad, she thought. He hadn't really got over losing her Mum. He must have been so worried.

"Hey Daddy. How are you doing?" Alan looked at his daughter and smiled. She was back with them, what more could he ask for?

"Hey yourself. You gave us quite a scare young lady. Now you have to do what the doctors say so we can get you home." Charlotte smiled. It was good to have her family there. "You have been working too hard."

"Charlie, you didn't fall down the stairs or anything, did you?" Charlotte shook her head.

"No, I was resting on the settee drinking cocoa and thinking about an early night. I'd had indigestion most of the day, but that wasn't unusual. Oh, and then the doorbell rang incessantly. It was James wanting to talk. I didn't let him in. I told him to make an arrangement to see me another time." Alan was furious.

"Does that man want to hurt you anymore?" Charlotte could see they all wanted to blame James.

"It really wasn't his fault. I'd had twinges all day but I thought it was indigestion. That's why I was having an early night. He left as soon as I told him to. I wonder if we should tell him I've lost his baby." Charlotte suddenly realised the enormity of what had happened. She burst out crying.

"He can wait. You get yourself fit first. Rest is what you need." Alan got up. It was time they left. Georgina had other ideas.

"I want to stay with Charlie. She needs me at the moment." Charlotte would have loved her sister to stay, normally, but she felt really tired. As if the nurse had heard her she came marching into the side-room and started waving her hand about.

"Come on now, past your bedtimes. This young lady needs her sleep. You can come back in the morning to see her. Off you go now." Charlotte liked her nurse. She took control without offence. Everyone kissed Charlotte and said goodbye. As they left the nurse told her that the doctor was on his way, just to check her over before she settled for the night. Charlotte could see a big clock on the wall saying the time was 3.30 a.m. She had been unconscious for hours. She assumed it was Saturday.

"Have I been out long?" The nurse tidied her bedding.

"You have been coming in and out since you arrived last night. You lost a lot of blood. But you're going to be fine now." She turned and smiled at Charlotte. "I'm Jenny, and will be here all night if there is anything you want, just press the button." She handed Charlotte the hand control and smiled at her. "I'm sorry you lost your little one. It was obviously meant to be, I always say. You are very young, plenty of time to make some more. Think of all the practice you can get in." She left Charlotte's room laughing aloud. Charlotte couldn't help herself. She smiled.

"Mrs Charlotte Whitfield?" A young, handsome doctor put his head around her door.

"Yes." Charlotte tried to push her hair back and hoped it looked better than it felt.

"Can I call you Charlotte?" Charlotte nodded. Anytime you like, she thought. I'll give you my mobile number. She smiled again. What was she doing? She had just lost a baby and was flirting with the doctor, in her mind. It had to be her hormones trying to get back to normal. "Right, your blood count is still very low so I've ordered a transfusion for you. You will probably be with us for a day or two, but you should feel more like your old self in no time after we've replaced the blood you lost. I'll set up the drip for you and then you can go to sleep." Jenny came back in with a bag of blood, while another nurse brought a drip stand in. They all checked Charlotte's name band with the blood and when they were happy they were putting it into the right patient, the doctor twiddled with a knob and it started dripping, very slowly. "I'll come and check you later. Goodnight Charlotte." He left with the auxiliary nurse. Jenny checked Charlotte was comfortable. Charlotte said she was.

"Before I go, would you like to hold your baby and say goodbye to her?" Charlotte looked totally confused. "The paramedics managed to retrieve the baby from your pyjama bottoms and wrapped her in a towel. Your baby was still attached to the placenta when they arrived. They managed to deliver your placenta as you were drifting in and out of consciousness." Charlotte was looking horrified. "She is perfectly formed, just very tiny. You don't have to see her if you don't want to. I find with my ladies that they all say thank you in the end. It helps you say goodbye to a little person that was part of you, even for such a short time." Charlotte took a deep breath. She would like to see her little girl. Jenny said she would go and get her.

Jenny came back a few minutes later holding a tiny baby in a pink blanket, with a little pink bonnet on its head. They had obviously been made for premature babies, or dollies, Charlotte thought, but what a lovely idea. Jenny was right. As she handed her to Charlotte, Charlotte saw that the little girl was perfect. Her skin was transparent, and she was so tiny, but her features were perfect. Jenny left Charlotte to say goodbye to her little daughter.

Charlotte held her little girl closely to her, as if trying to keep her warm.

"Hello." She wanted to think of an appropriate name for her. She quickly thought of a perfect name. "Hello Faith. I'm sorry we didn't have very long together, but you are going to see your nanny in heaven and she'll look after you." Charlotte was trying not to cry. "Goodnight little one, God Bless." She kissed her and cradled her until Jenny came back in. She leant over to take the baby off Charlotte. As she did so she handed Charlotte a photograph. It was a picture of Faith. She looked perfect, just asleep.

"Thank you so much Jenny. I really do feel better having said goodbye to her. I've called her Faith. Hopefully with a name like that Him up there will look after her for me." Jenny nodded.

"I'm sure you are right. It's a lovely name for a beautiful little girl." Jenny took Faith away and let Charlotte grieve in private.

In the morning Charlotte had a visit from a hospital counsellor.

"Hello dear. My name's Pippa Chapman, you can call me Pippa or Pip, whichever you like. I'm your hospital counsellor." Charlotte was none the wiser. Who or what is a hospital counsellor? She'd let the woman carry on. Perhaps she'll get the gist of her job description during conversation.

"Hello Pippa, pleased to meet you. I'm Charlotte." She shook Pippa's hand. She seemed a jolly sort.

"Now, you've got a little lady who needs help on her way to heaven, I hear." Ah, thought Charlotte, that type of counsellor. "Your options are a formal cremation or burial, which means your family and friends can join you. I have to tell you now, by law, neither are necessary. Your baby was born before the age of twenty-four weeks and therefore legally doesn't need birth or death certificates. The other option is our Angels baby garden. This is a plot of land behind the hospital that has been blessed and made into a beautiful garden and our miscarried babies are buried together there. Like I always say, all the babies taken too soon can play together and never be alone." Pippa took a photo out of her carpet bag, Charlotte couldn't help think of Mary Poppins at that moment, half expecting her to take out a coat stand, it was big enough. Pippa showed her the picture of the Angel garden. It was beautiful. It had an angel fountain in the middle with seats carved out of the surround. All around were little plots with teddies, colourful windmills and small balloons, toys and ornaments. It looked such a happy place.

Charlotte didn't need much time to think. She had already decided not to tell her family about Faith. Not in the immediate future anyway. So a funeral wasn't an option. She liked the idea of all the babies being together. She had heard that before the babies were a viable age they were classed as clinical waste and disposed of as such. Pippa told her things had moved on and if the hospital was able to, a more compassionate and sympathetic action was taken. Thus the wonderful garden, where anyone can visit and even leave little posies of flowers, or miniature balloons and teddies.

"So my dear, the Angel garden for little…?" Pippa hoped Charlotte had thought of a name for the little girl. It really did help to grieve a child rather than a foetus.

"Faith." Charlotte smiled. "I think that is a very lovely name for a baby going up to heaven." She surprised herself, having not been overly religious in the past. Something about the circumstances had made her feel comforted knowing Faith was going to be with the angels and her mother.

"Super, I'll organise that all for you. Once we have little Faith in her own plot in our garden I'll let you know. Did you want to be there for the interment?" Charlotte shook her head and wiped away a few tears. She had been so brave up until that point. Pippa realised Charlotte was only just holding it together. She felt awful spelling it all out to her, but it had to be done for closure. It was all to help the healing process.

It was time for her to wrap this visit up and let Charlotte get back to her grieving.

"I'll leave you in peace now then; with my heartfelt condolences to you my dear. Rest and vitamins are the only orders of the day, and of course time."

With Charlotte happy to leave everything in Pippa's hands, Pippa signed the form at the bottom of Charlotte's bed saying she had spoken to her and there was no need for a follow up, meaning Charlotte was sane, and gave her a card with her name and phone number on, in case she needed someone to talk to once she was home. With that she shook her hand and left. Charlotte took out the photograph of Faith and smiled. She would soon be with her mother. Bless them both, she thought and shut her eyes. She slept until lunchtime without waking. It felt a weight had been taken off her shoulders.

CHAPTER 5

Charlotte went home the next day, blood topped up. She had hidden the picture of Faith from everyone in a secret place. It would be difficult to keep a secret from Georgina, she never could, but maybe one day, when she was happily married with 2.4 children, she may confide in her and show her the picture of her beautiful niece, but she saw no point in upsetting her at present. The paramedics had been very discreet at the house, so apart from them and the nurses and doctor, no one even knew that the baby was found. It had been so small that it could easily have been mistakenly flushed down the toilet. Everything was so urgent that night and Charlotte was the number-one priority, Georgina hadn't even thought to look for it. Charlotte was glad that the paramedics had found her though. It was a wonderful thing being able to meet, cuddle and say goodbye to her little daughter, but it was to remain a secret. Charlotte had to remember in public she had to talk about her miscarriage of a foetus. It had to remain medical and impersonal.

She got straight back on the horse, phoning Bruce for an update on the website. Bruce had good news for her that gave her a boost. It looked like they may have to employ more people to handle the inundation of enquiries. She then telephoned her solicitors to see how her divorce was going, and the sale of her business. Again both issues were going extremely well. As nobody seemed to need her in the immediate future, she decided to buy a big bunch of flowers and go and talk to her mother. They now had a little secret between them and Charlotte wanted her mother to look after Faith for her.

She arrived at the graveyard, the sun was shining, and the grass had been freshly cut. She went straight over to her mother's grave and took out the dead flowers from the headstone vase and replaced them with the fresh ones. All the while she was telling her mum about Faith. She was a little sad that she couldn't have had Faith's ashes to sprinkle on her mum's grave, but that wouldn't have been practical. Individual foetus ashes wouldn't have been feasible to obtain. In any case, Faith wouldn't have wanted to be in a boring graveyard. She'd be much happier in a garden full of pretty flowers and balloons, with other babies to play with. Charlotte was actually convincing herself that she had done the right thing by talking aloud to her mother. She looked at her mother's headstone.

'INDIA PETERS Nee DE VILLIERS
TAKEN FROM HER LOVING FAMILY
AGED 50 YEARS.'

She was so young, thought Charlotte. She had so much

to give. Tears were streaming down her cheeks. She would never get over the premature death of her mother. It was getting a little easier to live with though. It had taken a long time for the family to get over India's death. She had gone to bed after a fantastic day celebrating her fiftieth birthday, with a headache. She had passed away by the morning, from a cranial aneurysm. Two weeks earlier she had been hit on the head by a golf ball while walking her Jack Russell, Patch, on the municipal golf course behind their home. It was a freak accident. They were near the boating lake, where Patch liked to swim. The ball had been sliced and lobbed over the protecting trees, the golfer not having a clue where his ball had landed. She lost consciousness for a short while. When India came to, a Good Samaritan had phoned for an ambulance and rung the number on the dog's collar. When Alan arrived at the local A & E the doctor told him that India had suffered a small crack in her skull, but the CT scan had shown no bleed. But just in case they would keep her in for a day or two to monitor her for concussion.

India was bright as a button the next day, but felt a little sick. They diagnosed mild concussion and watched her vital signs for another twenty-four hours. Then she went home. All she said of the incident was that it was a good job it hit her and not a child, and the poor golfer would have lost a stroke having to play a new ball!

She had been such an amazing woman. She'd had a privileged childhood. Her father, Francis, was 'something in the City', and her mother, Beatrice known affectionately as Bea, was a linguist and scholar. She had translated manuscripts for the British Museum. India had been a very welcome child, but came along in her mother and father's middle years. Her loving parents had died when India was in her teens, within a few years of each other. They had left her with a large trust fund which she spent very wisely using some to go to university to study Greek and classical Latin. Bea had given her daughter a thirst for knowledge; India's true love being classical literature. That was where Georgina got her passion. She used to sit for hours while her mother read aloud to her from books Bea had translated. The legacy India had left her girls was far more than just financial. They were a very close family made even closer by her passing.

Charlotte left the cemetery feeling stronger than she had felt for a while. Visiting and talking to her mother always had that effect on her. She walked away with determination. She had to tell James about her miscarriage, and there was no time like the present. She telephoned him from her car and arranged a neutral venue. As it was a bright sunny day Charlotte suggested the park, by the duck pond. There was a café there aptly named Swan Lake where they could have a civilised cup of coffee and an uninterrupted conversation.

He came within the hour. He could hear the urgency in Charlotte's voice and his hopes were raised. Perhaps his pleas through the door the other night hadn't fallen on deaf ears. He was getting more and more desperate by the day. He could not live with Libby for much longer. His hands were cracked from all the washing up, and he had the beginning of what he thought was housemaids knee.

She was sitting on the terrace of the café drinking a coffee. It was like travel sickness, as soon as she lost the baby she lost the sickness feeling, and now savoured her coffee as she had done before. He watched her from a distance before she could see him. He realised what an absolute idiot he'd been. For all Libby's glitter and grandeur, albeit fake, Charlotte exuded plain beauty and intelligence. He had to win her back. He moved into her vision, she smiled.

"Ah, you've got a coffee. Would you like another?" James leaned over and kissed her cheek.

"No thank you. I'm enjoying this one more than you will ever know." James wasn't sure what she meant but disappeared into the café to get a coffee for himself. By the time he came out Charlotte had changed her demeanour. She looked extremely serious. It made James feel very uncomfortable.

"I'm sorry James, but I will come straight to the point as there is no easy way of telling you this, but I lost our baby a few days ago." James was shocked. His first thought was how careless, how can you lose something that was inside you. Then the full meaning dawned on him. He looked devastated. Charlotte put her hand on his. They sat there for a while in companionable silence. Charlotte wouldn't have felt so sorry for him if she could read his mind. Of course James was devastated, but not for the loss of the baby, but for his lost leverage to get back into the family fold. Charlotte misread his grief.

"I'm so sorry James." He looked up at Charlotte. She was crying. Perhaps all wasn't lost after all. He could play the sympathy card. He got up and put his arms around Charlotte.

"You poor thing. You should have phoned me sooner. You shouldn't have had to go through that on your own." She pushed him away, gently and fished for a tissue from her handbag.

"I wasn't alone, I had my family with me." She didn't mean to be brutal, but he had to realise that she had moved on. He sat back down and tried another approach.

"Are you ok? Was it awful?" Charlotte didn't want him to know too much.

"It wasn't the best time of my life, but it is over now and I'm moving on. One day the timing will be right and hopefully I can have another baby, but the timing wasn't right and perhaps someone was trying to tell us that." James couldn't leave it there.

"We could try again, Charlotte. I've missed you so much. I made such a bad mistake and I want to come home. You need me as much as I need you. For better for worse, in sickness and in health." He smiled at her.

"*NOW* you remember your wedding vows. You really are a piece of work James. Just because I'm tearful at the moment, with my hormones trying to get back to normal, I'm not stupid. I know you are not happy with Libby, but you made your choice. You don't want to come back to me out of love or remorse. You want somewhere to live away from the luscious Libby. Well, it won't be with me." James was actually speechless. She had entirely read him brilliantly. He had the good grace to lower his head and look slightly contrite. Charlotte looked at him. Had she been a little harsh? Probably, but he did ask for it. She took a deep breath. "There is something I can do for you, but you must promise to stop this nonsense of thinking we could ever get back together." James looked up and nodded. "Well, with the sale of the business and being the only B share holder, you will get dividends which would be enough for a month or two's rent for a flat. Unfortunately, you may have to wait before the money is in the bank." He looked mortified that he would have to stay with Libby for a few more months; days would be all he could stand. "Of course, I could take some money out of my trust fund to cover you until it all goes through." James jumped up off his seat and tried to hug Charlotte. She pushed him away, not quite so gently as the first time. "I have a proposition for you. I will give you a glowing reference and enough money to rent a flat for six months at which time you should be employed. After all you are brilliant at your job. I'll let you continue your golf club membership, which I still pay for, until the end of the year. At least you should be able to meet new clients there and get some private jobs for your web designs." James wasn't happy but had to admit she was being very generous. He'd been so stupid, what was that old saying, 'never bite the hand that feeds you?' How true.

"I agree. How long before I can start looking for a flat?" To the point –Charlotte liked that. He had made the whole arrangement feel like a business deal.

"I'll place some money into your account this afternoon, the rest is up to you." She stood up and extended her hand. He shook it. "You'll be hearing from my solicitor about the finalisation of the divorce proceedings, apart from that I'm sure there are no other matters, so I shall say goodbye James. Oh, and good luck." She walked away with the feeling that another door had closed. Loose ends tied up. The future now primed and ready to go. She quickened her pace, wanting her future to start as soon as possible.

Bruce popped in on his way home from golf. Charlotte looked shattered. She was still doing too much, he thought. He needed some papers signed for the accountant, but looking at her he decided they could wait. He'd come back tomorrow. Charlotte insisted he came in. He went to the kitchen and put the kettle on. Charlotte had been sending money through to James' account online. She was feeling a little lonely. Bruce had come just in time. He always seemed to brighten her day. She hoped the feeling was reciprocated. While he was in the kitchen making a pot of tea his phone rang.

"It's Libby. I'll leave it. I'm not in the mood for an argument." He made the tea and had ignored the phone three more times. On the fourth he decided it had to be urgent or she would have given up. He answered it. Libby was in a state. James had gone upstairs after he'd received an email from his bank and packed his things and had just left. Bruce felt a little sorry for her. He told her to calm down and he'd pop round in the morning to check on her. He was too good for her, Charlotte thought. He explained what had happened to Charlotte.

"Ah, the money had gone in then. I knew he'd do something like that, just not so soon. He really is a bastard." Charlotte couldn't believe James had stooped so low.

"I knew he was desperate, but even Libby didn't deserve that." Or did she?

"You have a very short memory." Bruce told her. "Come on, put your shoes on, I'm taking you out for dinner." There was no need to dress up; they were only going to the local Pizzeria round the corner. Charlotte realised how brilliant Bruce had been all the way through. Considering his marriage had fallen apart, he was always more worried about Charlotte. It hadn't gone unnoticed. During the meal she thanked him. They had both got a little tipsy; it'd been weeks since Charlotte had had that amount of alcohol.

"Bruce, you are a man in a million. Do you know that?" Bruce smiled. Charlotte was getting back to her old self. He knew it was mainly alcohol talking, but she was having a good time, which was the purpose of the exercise. Before he could answer her, she carried on. "I am very fond of you Bruce, always have been. Libby is an idiot and so is James, come to that. But Libby had you, stupid, stupid woman. Fancy letting a gem like you go." She hiccupped. Bruce laughed. Charlotte laughed too.

"Well I think James is as much an idiot. They deserved each other." He looked into Charlotte's eyes. "We will be ok, Charlotte. For a wee while it will be hard, but we'll look back at this time and think what tossers they both were." Charlotte burst out laughing. Bruce joined her. People looked over and smiled at the lovely couple sharing a joke in the corner.

"I love you Bruce Gordon. You make me laugh." Well, thought Bruce, if that was every woman's prerequisite to love it's a wonder he hasn't got a queue of women lining up to marry him. Funny thing he thought, Libby didn't laugh much at all. She tutted a lot, but laughter failed to brighten her world. Shame, he thought. She'd be a much happier person if she'd just let go of her emotions once in a while. Charlotte yawned. It was time to get her home.

"Charlotte, it's been a lovely evening, but I think it's time to go home. Don't you?" Charlotte had to agree. She felt a little light-headed and as the alcohol was wearing off tiredness was flooding in with a vengeance.

"You are right, as usual Bruce. I've had such a nice time. This has been the nicest evening I've had since." She thought for a moment. "Since the last one I had with you." She couldn't remember a nice night with James for a long time. Bruce got the bill and helped Charlotte home.

More was said than should have been that night, but Charlotte hoped Bruce had been as drunk as she was to remember any of it in the morning. As a gentleman, he'd not mention it the next day, unless she brought it up.

He slept in the spare room at Charlotte's insistence. He couldn't drive back to his flat in the state he was in. By the time Charlotte had showered and got down to the kitchen, Bruce had made their breakfast of homemade Scottish pancakes with golden syrup. She could get used to that. She still couldn't understand why Libby swapped Bruce for James.

Bruce remembered mentioning to Libby, a few months before they split up, that the take-away web business was worth nearly £2 million if it was sold. Libby probably assumed that the business was James' as Charlotte was never one to blow her own trumpet. She must have given James such a hard time once she realised he wasn't worth much.

Charlotte laughed as she said Libby would be dead gutted if it were Bruce who became the millionaire. Charlotte knew it was possible; Bruce just loved working with Charlotte for the sake of being with her most days.

Bruce went round to see Libby that morning. She was distraught. She wanted Bruce back. He'd never treated her like James. He had been a wonderful husband. She didn't understand why he hadn't fought for her. Bruce had to admit that the feelings he had for Libby, although sympathetic, were also mainly pity. She got very angry and threw the nearest thing at him. It was a lamp, a 1920s bronze oil lamp converted to electric, another piece of his Scottish history. Bruce just managed to catch it although it was heavy and was tempted to throw it back. Instead he unplugged it and took it with him out of the door. He had always loved that lamp and Libby didn't deserve it.

CHAPTER 6

Georgina finally handed in her notice, with effect at the end of the school year, only two months away. In the meantime, she waded through the literary work being downloaded onto their website and categorising them into their relevant genres. She loved every minute of it. Some novels were absolute rubbish, but she found a couple which were wonderful and couldn't understand why they hadn't been published. She decided with Charlotte that the shortlisted ones she thought had a chance, would be send directly to publishing houses as a free agent. If they were accepted the company would get a commission fee and the authors would get a book deal. Georgina couldn't wait to work full-time at a job that was actually made for her. What a clever sister she had.

Three days after leaving the hospital Charlotte received a telephone call.

"Hello, Charlotte?" Charlotte recognised the voice but could not place it.

"Yes, this is Charlotte." She heard a lot of rustling and a big sigh, and then it came to her. The energy that was transferring down the phone meant it could only be one person.

"Pippa Chapman here. How are you doing?" Not giving Charlotte time to reply she went straight into the reason for her call. *"Just to let you know that your beautiful daughter, Faith, is with the Angels. She has a lovely position next to a naughty little rascal called Sebastian and opposite another little angel called Grace. I have pictures for you, if you'd like to give me your email address I'll attempt to send them. Not exactly brilliant at this technology lark, but I'll give it a go!"* Charlotte recited her email address to Pippa and thanked her for doing all the arrangements for her. *"Not at all, my pleasure. One more thing before I go, there is room on her little plot for some sort of plaque or stone if you would like to put one on. The stonemason in North Street usually does them, quite beautifully in my opinion. Totally up to you my dear. If you visit the garden you can see what other Mummies and Daddies have done and get some ideas. God Bless you my dear. Goodbye."* Without further ado, she was gone. That was the sort of phone call Charlotte liked. Pippa was to the point, saying what needed to be said and no more. Charlotte thought she must remember to put her on this year's Christmas card list. She smiled to herself. Some people just suited their jobs to a T.

Charlotte checked her emails, nothing from Pippa yet, she'd check again later but she had to go to see her father who'd rung that morning with a very bad cold. He'd told her not to fuss, but asked her if she could just pop in with some milk and a newspaper if she was passing. She'd done some shopping for him on her way to make sure he rested and had easy to cook food. On the top of her list was tomato soup, her mother's cure for any ailment.

"Cooee, Daddy?" She took the shopping straight into his kitchen. "I'll put the kettle on and make us a nice cup of coffee." Alan had heard her car pull up and came downstairs. He stood in the kitchen doorway and smiled to himself. Charlotte was the image of her mother at that age. It was a comfort to him in a way. Funny though, Georgie was more like her mother in personality and Charlie was definitely her father's daughter. "Oh, there you are. I've bought you a few bits and pieces so you won't have to go out until you're feeling better."

"You should be spoiling yourself, not me. I'm made of strong stuff you know." At that he exploded into a coughing fit. Charlotte looked at him and laughed. She knew she shouldn't but he asked for it.

"Go and sit in the living room and I'll bring you a coffee and a bun with your newspaper." He did as he was told, he didn't have the energy to argue, and if he was honest, he didn't want to either. Charlotte was a force to be reckoned with once she was in control and Alan knew it was for his own good. It was actually nice to have someone taking care of him he'd missed that when his dear wife passed on. He wasn't ungrateful to his lovely daughters, they were very caring and attentive, but it wasn't the same. Charlotte brought in a tray with two coffees, his newspaper and a surprise on a plate.

"You naughty girl. You know I can't resist a custard

slice." He grinned up at her. She had used the ploy her mother used when her dad was poorly. He loved custard slices. Charlotte had treated herself to a chocolate éclair, her favourite. She needed to put on some weight and decided to do it with a little naughtiness thrown in. They sat together chatting while they ate their treats. Charlotte thought her father looked better already. She looked at her watch.

"You get off when you've finished your coffee. I know you have things to do. I'll be fine. You look after yourself. You still look a little peaky to me. Is everything all right now? You know, back to normal?" He found it difficult to talk about ladies' things, like most men, but he wanted to make sure she was ok.

"I'm fine, Daddy. It wasn't meant to be and I've still got plenty of time to make you a granddad so stop worrying." She got up and went over to him. She bent down and kissed his forehead. He waved her away.

"Go, go, go, you do not need a cold at the moment. Thank you for my shopping and the custard slice. I'll have the tomato soup for lunch and should be right as rain in no time!" He laughed and she joined him. At that moment she felt very lucky having her dad still in her life. She would love to show him the picture of his granddaughter, but it wasn't the right time. It was all far too raw still. One day will be right; she'd wait for that day.

She took the coffee tray into the kitchen and stacked the dishwasher, poured the soup into a saucepan and put it on the stove. Placed a couple of slices of bread in the toaster, said her goodbyes and left. She looked again at her watch and decided to go home and check her emails. She was anxious to see her little girl's resting place.

Unknown to Charlotte, she was being followed. She arrived home and was getting out of her car when a hand pulled her car door open. She looked up to see James' face staring down at her. Charlotte felt very uncomfortable.

"James stop staring at me like that, you are freaking me out. What do you want anyway?" James stood back while Charlotte got out of her car.

"I know you told me to stop pestering you, but I've left Libby. It was a dreadful mistake. Oh Charlotte, what have I done to us?" He tried to get close to her, but she pushed a shopping bag between them.

"James, for the last time, there is no 'us'."

When did Charlotte get so hard, he wondered. He'd have to be more convincing.

"There could be if you let me make it up to you. I'm so sorry Charlie. It was a huge error of judgement on my part, but I never stopped loving you, never." She was getting very worried. James seemed to be acting weird. It was too early for alcohol to be involved.

"James, will you please leave. We had an agreement and if you carry on like this I will put a stop on the direct debit payments. Now please go and we will say no more about this little outburst." She was sounding a lot stronger than she was feeling. She had worked out an escape route while she was talking. If she could get James behind her car she had a clear run up to her front door. James changed tactics.

"Ok I'll go." He turned to leave, then over his shoulder he asked. "By the way, how's it working out with Bruce?" Charlotte noticed the smirk on James' face.

"Our working arrangement seems to be going very well.

He grasps what I want and manages to implement ideas given to him very quickly." James was now facing Charlotte. He still had an inane grin on his face.

"So, he knows what you want and how to please you then?" James was playing with innuendos to annoy Charlotte. She just tutted and shook her head.

"Poor James, still the school boy. In grownup land, where people can have adult conversations, you'd struggle. But I'll come into your playground for a moment. Let's get two things clear. Firstly, you shattered my faith in men. Secondly you took a wonderful man's life, put it in a shredder and he was too much of a gentleman to give you what you deserved. But now, we've both picked up the pieces, and have come out the other side with an amazing new venture. If you try in any way to demean or disparage our hard work, I will personally hit you where it will well and truly hurt, in your pocket." James realised that she wasn't bluffing. She had been more than generous with his settlement. "And on that note, goodbye James." She walked steadily up her driveway, hoping he wouldn't follow her. She managed to put the key in her lock and turn it. James knew he'd blown it. He had nothing else to lose.

"Charlotte, wait." He could see her turn the key and open the outer door. If she got into the lobby he'd have no chance of talking to her. He sprinted up the driveway and managed to get his foot in the door before she could close it. She was now very scared.

"Don't ignore me," he shouted. He was furious. Charlotte decided to match like for like.

"Don't you dare speak to me in that tone. Go home James." She tried to force his foot out with her own.

"I have no home. You are in it. A chap makes *one* mistake and is expected to pay for it forever. It just shows me that you never loved me in the first place, otherwise you would have forgiven me by now." There was a loud cough from behind James. He turned round to see Bruce standing there.

"You ok Charlotte?" She nodded. "Would you be so kind as to remove your foot from the door, James?" James did as he was told, a broken man, he had no fight left in him. "Now, say goodbye to Charlotte and be on your way, there's a good chap." James turned to Charlotte and managed a very quiet 'goodbye'. Charlotte smiled at him.

"Goodbye James. Take care of yourself." She was feeling very sorry for him. She actually pitied him for being such a spineless wimp, although at that moment was glad of it. Bruce escorted him down the driveway and into his car. James drove away. Charlotte ran down the drive.

"Thank you so much Bruce. I was really getting scared." Bruce put his arms around her and after the last ten minutes of fear, she surrendered into them. It felt so natural.

"I've just come from Libby. She'd had a massive fight with James and it ended up with her telling James he owed her for room and board, and half the bills since he'd been living there. I had an inkling he would be after you for more money. I'm glad I decided to take the long way home to check on you." So was Charlotte.

"Thank you for always being there for me Bruce." Charlotte looked up at him and smiled.

"You are very welcome." Bruce smiled back and an invisible bond seemed to be working its magic between them. Charlotte thought it was probably just a deepening friendship due to the pair of them going through the same trauma in their lives but she also wondered if it was something more.

James was still preying on Charlotte's mind the following day. She'd made him financially sound for the time being, but his mental state was very worrying. She knew it wasn't her problem, but she felt she had to help him. She needed to make him get into a positive mindset otherwise no matter how much money was thrown at him it would be wasted. She wanted to move on in her life so everything had to be stable in his. He was a loose cannon at the moment and needed to be steered into a new direction. If Bruce could read her thoughts he would be angry. The problem was that James had been a good husband up until the floosy known as 'her ex-best-friend' had turned him into a gigolo of sorts and Charlotte felt she owed it to their original marriage vows to help him back into the normal world and out of his dangerous spiral of unaccountability. Remembering the old James helped her with her sense of purpose. She'd organise a mutual venue, perhaps a restaurant where there were lots of people, and hopefully get through to him that life was not over just because they were no longer together.

On refection, as she picked up her phone, she wondered if she was not just stirring a hornet's nest. But she decided she couldn't let things stay as they were. She would talk to him and give him advice on how to get his life back on track. After all there was no one else he could turn to. He'd alienated most of their friends and he had no immediate family.

"Hello, James?" Thinking quickly she had to make sure he didn't think this was a date. "It's Charlie."

"I can see it's you! How lovely to hear your voice. Are you ok?" James couldn't believe after his behaviour the day before that she was still talking to him.

"We need to meet to finalise things. I feel too much has not been said and therefore misunderstandings are keeping us both from moving on. I wondered if you were free tomorrow we could perhaps have a bite to eat and clear the air at the same time." Was that non-committal enough? Did it sound business like? She thought it did, but there was no telling what James thought. She found it impossible to read him these days.

"What a swell idea." Charlotte shuddered. That was a Libby-ism and she hated it. They were not American. *"You say where and when and I'll be there."*

Charlotte had given it a lot of thought. She didn't want anywhere romantic, but she needed somewhere where they could hear themselves talking. That ruled out most Italian restaurants. She had decided on a pub. They could have a quiet corner but in very public view. "I'll meet you at the Durley Inn, at seven o'clock tomorrow evening."

"It's a date!" James said jovially.

"Under no circumstances is it a 'date' James. You can knock that idea out of your head right now, or I will cancel the 'meeting'." She emphasised the word meeting to put her point across.

"Only kidding. Looking forward to our 'meeting' tomorrow. See you at seven. Bye Charlie." The line went dead. Charlotte was having second thoughts already. Maybe she should tell George, or Tom but definitely not Bruce. She

felt, for some unknown reason, that she was betraying Bruce. But she believed it was the only possible course of action to lay all her demons i.e. Libby and James, to rest.

She checked her emails on her phone and there was one from Pippa, with five attachments. Well done Pippa she thought and smiled. It had taken Pippa nearly twenty-four hours to master sending attachments, but she had got there. Charlotte went to the breakfast table and opened her iPad. She opened each attachment and tears were running down her cheeks. They were beautiful. The first was of Faith, in a little white bonnet and snuggled up in a white shawl. She looked like she was sleeping. The second was of a small white cardboard box with a ribbon tied around it and a little teddy bear label tied on with the words "*Faith, playing with the angels*". The third was of the beautiful garden and the small space that had been designated for Faith. It was exactly where Pippa said it was. It was next to a little plot marked with a stone car with the name Sebastian etched in the registration plate. How clever she thought. The fourth was Faith's plot after she had been interred. The soil was freshly tilled and a little temporary wooden cross had been put on it with Faith's name written on it in ink. The fifth was one taken from a distance showing all the beautiful little plots looking so cared for with teddies and windmills and flowers in abundance. Charlotte wiped her eyes and decided that she needed to get a stone as soon as possible to make Faith's spot as pretty as the others. She had decided on a stone in the shape of a little baby lying cosily in a pillow. She'd seen it on the stonemason's website and thought it very apt. She'd add a plaque saying 'Faith Peters

– *Sweet Dreams Little Angel'*. She carefully put the photos into a new folder marked 'Darling Faith', wiped her eyes for the final time, turned off her iPad, collected her keys and drove to the stonemasons to bring to a close another part of her life; Faith, gone but never forgotten.

Bruce was waiting for her when she got home. She really wanted to explain to him why she was meeting James, but didn't know how to without feeling she was letting him down. He took it out of her hands.

"I'm meeting Libby tomorrow night. We need to get things thrashed out and concluded before we can both move on." Charlotte was grinning. "And you are finding it amusing because?" Charlotte breathed a sigh of relief.

"I am doing exactly the same thing with James tomorrow night." Bruce smiled. But then his brow furrowed with doubt. Was that wise? He didn't want to frighten Charlotte, but on James's recent behaviour he wasn't sure she was doing the right thing. He can handle Libby but James was volatile at the moment.

"Will you be alone?" Charlotte could see the concern in Bruce's face.

"I was going to tell Tom to be on stand-by in case things got nasty. But then I thought if I met him in a public place I'd be safe." Bruce still looked worried. "You're not so sure?" Charlotte had her own doubts too. "Perhaps we could go as a foursome." They both laughed, strained, but slightly more relaxed.

"Where are you meeting him?" Bruce had to respect Charlotte's decisions; it wasn't his place to tell her what an eejit he thought she was being. James had proved himself to be a spineless creature, of late, and he wouldn't put it passed him to thump a woman in the frame of mind he was in at that moment.

"Well I thought a restaurant may give him the wrong idea, so we're meeting at the Durley Inn, by the seafront, hopefully the bracing wind will clear our heads. I've told him seven o'clock." It was Bruce's turn to smile.

"I had the same idea. I thought a pub the better option. The Durley Inn passed through my mind, but I settled on The Beehive. It's usually full of the older members of the village on weeknights and I'm hoping that Libby will be on her best behaviour in front of them." They both chuckled knowingly. Charlotte knew only too well how much Libby relied on the people of the village thinking she was a delightful woman, always baking for the Church fete. The truth be known, she bought them from a family bakers in the next town and took off all their wrapping, substituting it with baking parchment. "I hope you don't think I'm interfering in your life, but I'd feel happier if you check-in with me from time to time during the evening, just to let me know you are ok. I'm sure he'll behave, but please humour me." Charlotte's heart skipped a beat. Bruce was so caring and thoughtful. She wanted to stretch up and kiss him. Surely her hormones should be back to normal by now, she thought. "Just a quick text will do."' Bruce had misunderstood her delay in answering. After all she was his boss. He didn't want to overstep the mark. But he cared for her.

"I will humour you Bruce. Thank you for caring. I hope Libby behaves for you. The sooner we get those two sorted the sooner we can get on with our lives." Maybe together she thought. Charlotte noticed Bruce's frown disappear. Perhaps he was thinking the same as her.

CHAPTER 7

Bruce was not looking forward to seeing Libby. She'd been weeping and wailing on his voicemail for the past twenty-four hours and it was getting very wearing. He had to be strong. He was finally enjoying his new life and Libby was well and truly in his past, but he had to convince her of that. He was still worried about Charlotte's meeting with James and would like to wrap up his dinner with his ex-wife as soon as politely possible. He sent a text to Charlotte wishing her luck and telling her to stay strong. He realised the irony in his message and smiled. That evening he was going to have to practice what he preached.

Charlotte was about to go out of the door to her dreaded meeting with her ex-husband when her phone beeped. She looked at it and saw it was a message from Bruce.

*"Best of luck tonight, and don't take any bullsh*t from him."* She had to smile. What part of the word was one

asterisk going to screen? He was sweet. *"Stay strong and resolute. Your life is so much better now; don't let him change your mind! Keep safe. Bruce X"* Her smile changed to a slight worried frown. She realised that James was unpredictable and Bruce was just trying to warn her to be on her guard, but she saw no other choice. She hadn't told her sister where she was going, nor her father, for the same reason – they would have stopped her. Either that or gone with her. She had to do this alone. After all James was a coward and a wimp of late, she really didn't see the necessity of over reacting. With that thought she locked up the house and set off on her mission to get closure on her former life with James.

James was pacing up and down the promenade trying to work out how he was going to play the evening to his satisfaction. He really didn't want to blow it. He had money to keep him for a few months but he needed security for a lot longer than that. He needed Charlotte and her brain as well as her wealth. He had an ace up his sleeve, literally. He was wearing the cuff links she bought him for their engagement party, with CP (heart) JW engraved on them. Flash of genius, he thought. Get her mind back to happier days and try to keep it there.

"Hello James, hope you haven't been waiting long. Shall we go in?" She caught him off guard. He'd been so engrossed in his planning he'd not noticed her car pull into the carpark. He was slightly off footed and she'd taken control. He'd have to pay more attention or his plans will disintegrate before he had time to execute them.

"No, I haven't been here long." He hoped lightning wouldn't strike him down for that lie. He'd been there an hour, clearing his head and psyching himself up. "You are looking lovely tonight. Have you done something new with your hair?" Careful, he thought, don't want to lay it on too thick. He smiled at her.

Charlotte wanted to heave. She really didn't like the new James. He was being very creepy. She preferred it when he paid her no attention at all, rather than this fake attentiveness.

"I booked us a table." She looked at her watch. "It should be ready for us." She stopped at the sign, *'Please wait to be seated'*, and looked around for a member of staff. Luckily for her it was busy, so more chance of James behaving himself. A spotty youth came towards them. He checked the diary and grabbed two menus and asked them to follow him. As planned, he showed them into a corner, just off the main area without the sea views. Not as popular, but it suited Charlotte, far enough away to talk privately but near enough to the throng if required. James immediately took off his jacket and made a show of pulling his sleeves down with his cufflinks prominent. Charlotte had noticed the ploy and was getting angry. If he really thought he could win his way back into her life with old memories of happier times he must think she was a Stepford wife. "A little overdressed for a pub, aren't you?" She picked up the menu and perused it.

James gritted his teeth. That would have worked in the movies. What a hard bitch Charlotte had become. "Shall we have a bottle of wine?" Perhaps he can get her to relax with alcohol.

"I'm driving James. I'll have a small white wine spritzer though. You'll probably be quicker fetching it from the bar." He took the hint and walked over to the nice young barmaid behind the bar. Charlotte took the opportunity of checking her phone. She had felt it vibrate a few minutes previously. It was Bruce.

"How's your evening going? Libby has gone to the loo to powder her nose! She seems to have rubbed her eyes raw, but I'm not falling for it! When did I get so hard? ;-)" Charlotte looked up and could see James flirting with the barmaid. She started texting.

"I'm being hard too! Get us!! He's at the bar ordering drinks at the moment, flirting with the barmaid. My resolve is getting stronger with each of her giggles!! Over and out!" James was on his way back to the table.

"I remembered you liked it with soda not lemonade. Cheers." He chinked his beer onto her wine glass.

"Cheers. I think I might have the steak and ale pie with chips. I fancy something naughty." She regretted her words as soon as they had spoken. James looked up at her and smiled. Charlotte sighed. He really was a schoolboy at heart. She used to find it so endearing but now it was rather irritating. She needed to cut the evening short. Her hand waved in front of a waitress and she managed to get her attention. "I'd like the steak and ale pie with a side of chips please." The waitress tapped her order into an electronic gadget and then looked at James.

"What would you recommend?" he asked her with a grin on his face.

"Depends what you like to eat, sir." Good girl, thought Charlotte. She must be so used to lecherous males in pubs. James briefly scanned the menu.

"I'll have the same as the lady. Thank you." Charlotte rolled her eyes. He was being particularly trying, but she mustn't let him get to her. The waitress tapped his order into her device, collected their menus and walked off.

James asked Charlotte how everyone was. They made polite conversation without innuendos all through dinner. Charlotte could see the anxiety on James's face, but he was being very restrained.

Coffee was ordered and Charlotte had asked for the bill at the same time. She decided it was time to end the evening.

"Well James, this has been civil. I hope the civility will carry on after the divorce is through." James stared at her without saying a word. She felt very uncomfortable. She couldn't read his expression, as he didn't have one. His face was blank. She carried on. "You should have a tidy sum in your bank within the next few months. The sale price went far beyond my expectations so as a shareholder you have done jolly well." His face hadn't changed and she was now getting worried. Was he going to explode or stay comatose? She checked the bill and put down the cash including the tip. If she paid by card she could be waiting for eternity. Her coffee was finished and there was no reason to prolong the evening any longer. "I'll say goodbye then. I hope everything works out well for you James, I really do." She got up and picked up her bag. Her car keys were in the front pocket so she took them out. His eyes had followed her up, but his head had stayed in the same position. She waited for him to say something, but he didn't. She put up her hand and did a little wave. "Ciao." Feeling very apprehensive she took her phone out of her pocket as she made her way to the carpark. As soon as she was in the car she'd text Bruce to see how his evening had gone and see if he fancied a nightcap. They could compare notes. James had been quite normal at the beginning of the evening but he was now particularly odd. She quickened her pace. The waves were making a noise in the background so she couldn't hear the footsteps quickening behind her.

"Charlotte, wait." She turned around and saw James standing behind her. The lighting wasn't great and the moon was behind him, making it difficult to see his facial expression. She had two choices, stand and talk or turn and run. She chose the latter. She turned and was about to dash to her car when a very determined hand had her by the shoulder. "Do not run away from me." James swung her round to face him. She didn't need to see his expression. She could hear his deep breathing and almost feel the heat coming from his anger. She had to bluff it out. There were no people around she could call for help. The sea would have drowned her voice in any case.

"How dare you touch me. You lost that right when you first fondled Libby." He loosened his grip but didn't let go.

"Get over it. That relationship is dead. I love you Charlotte, I always have. You and I are soul mates. You can't annul our marriage after one simple mistake. I'm a chap, for goodness sake. If a woman throws herself at me it'd be rude to push her off." He was laughing almost dementedly. "It was Libby's fault." He had stopped laughing and was now back in schoolboy mode. "I admit I made a huge error of judgement, but why can't you forgive me? I need you Charlie. I have no one else. I'm lost without you. Please can we start again?" He sniffed for effect. Charlotte felt like smiling, but didn't. The fake sobbing was not going to work. Perhaps it had been the loss of her baby, or the friendship with Bruce that had made her determined. Whatever it was it helped her stay steadfast and strong.

"James, you and I know that it is the comfortable life you miss. You could have that with someone else if you chose more wisely. Be honest with yourself James. You are a good man and could be an amazing father and husband, but not with me. Admit it to yourself and you will find it easier to move on." Charlotte hadn't noticed that James had let go of her sometime during her dialogue. She was standing talking to him of her own volition, which made her feel even stronger. She totally turned the tables on him and put her hand on his shoulder. "I will still be here James, if you need any business advice or help, but it will have to be by appointment in the future, not just turning up as and when. Is that fair?" He looked totally defeated. She wanted to hug him but knew that would undo the whole last ten minutes. Instead she patted him on the back. "You have a wonderful skill James, that will get you clients and a future. You do not need me anymore. Just believe in yourself." She was beginning to feel like a motivational guru. Whatever had sunk in was working. He physically straightened and nodded.

"I am bloody good at developing software, look how much we've made on our last venture." Charlotte had to admit, he'd done a good job. He turned to go. "It's been a good evening Charlie. Let's not say goodbye, but adieu." He waved his hand and walked off into the darkness. Charlotte hoped he had finally moved on, time would tell.

By the time Charlotte had got up, on that very sunny morning, the postman had already been. She'd had a very late meeting with Bruce and George the night before which had gone on into 'the wee small hours' as Bruce had pointed out before they left. The new venture was doing so well. George was now working full time on the project and that was making an amazing difference in the turnover. The children at her school were very sad to see one of their favourite teachers leave, and she was inundated with gifts and cards at the end of the school term.

The evening meeting went very well. Charlotte didn't act like the boss. She encouraged them all to have equal responsibility in their own areas of expertise. She was obviously in charge over all, but as there were three of them it was very convenient for voting purposes. They had to decide whether to take literallyworms.co.uk public. They thrashed out the pros and cons and decided to wait until they had been running for one year and make a more informed decision then.

Charlotte put the kettle on and opened her post. There was a letter from Jeremy, enclosed with it was her decree nisi. She hadn't appeared in court but all seemed to go smoothly according to Jeremy. She breathed a sigh of relief. She wasn't sure if James was going to defend it or protest in any way. Obviously he hadn't. Jeremy was going to apply for the decree absolute in six weeks' time, when she would then be rid of James forever. He had been remarkably quiet of late. According to Bruce, Libby had heard he had another woman, but that could just be sour grapes on her part. She felt a weight had been lifted from her shoulders.

What no one knew was that James had been working very hard at his new business. He had put many feelers out at the Golf Club and they had resulted in several jobs, mainly setting up new websites for people who needed quick and cheap advertising for their companies. It wasn't what he enjoyed doing, there was no challenge there for him. He could set up websites in his sleep. He needed a project like Charlotte's. Bruce was probably mucking it up; he didn't have the same skills as James. He played it too safe. James, on the other hand, had the drive, the knowhow and the cutting-edge ideas. Or he'd like to think he had. Unfortunately, he was also full of bitterness and jealousy, which meant that anything he put his mind to wasn't getting one hundred per cent attention.

He started to get emails from disgruntled clients. A lot of the websites were crashing, or just weren't allowing information to go onto them. Silly mistakes and shortcuts had been made but James didn't seem too bothered, he'd been paid. Unfortunately the Golf Club was a close-knit community, the 'old boy network' at its best. He was starting to get a bad reputation and it was snowballing fast. To the point where he was inundated with cancellations even on the work he had started, which meant no payment.

He had been living a good life since he'd left Libby, with proceeds from Charlotte. Regrettably for James, it was running out. He'd been stupid. He realised that too late. He'd also managed to fit in a fling with the Pro's wife and she was getting a little too demanding. He decided to keep a low profile at the Club and therefore work was drying up from all fronts. He needed money. His first thought was Charlotte. He'd given her space, but maybe now was the time to try and get back into her good books. She must have missed him. He'd opened his post that day and found the decree nisi. He knew she would have received hers too. Perhaps it was the time to make contact. Make sure she was ok. Play the worried ex. It could work.

Charlotte had just cleared the mess up from the night before when the phone rang. She looked at the caller ID and was surprised to see it was James. Of course, she thought, he'd have received his decree nisi that morning too. She wondered what he wanted. Curiosity made her answer.

"Hello James. How are you?" She stretched over the table to grab her coffee; she felt it could be a long conversation.

"Hi Charlie. I'm fine, thank you. Just wondered how you were. I expect you got the solicitors letter this morning? Just making sure everything was ok." He needed to steer her round to a meeting. *"Do you fancy a coffee?"* 'Please' he thought, but didn't want to sound desperate. *"I thought we could compare notes and make sure we were both happy with the documents before they are finalised."*

"I think they are self-explanatory James. I see no need to look at them further." She felt harsh, but knew where it would lead if she had to meet up with him. Just when she thought he'd moved on too. Oh well, she'd have to nip any thoughts of a meeting in the bud. "I hear on the grapevine that your business venture has done exceedingly well. I knew it would once you put your mind to it." Before James could answer Charlotte hurried on. "Anyway James, as nice as it is to catch up, I'm afraid I have a meeting in twenty minutes and I haven't even put my face on yet. Goodbye James, keep up the good work." James was fuming. He drew breath to respond only to realise the phone had gone dead.

How dare she. Patronising bitch, he thought. What on earth did he ever see in her? But he knew that he had loved her, once. It had also helped that he had got the whole package in his relationship with her. He had a job, money in his bank account, a lovely home, good cooked meals, clothes washed and ironed and ready to wear at all times, membership to the most prestigious golf club in the area, to name but a few attributes to becoming Charlotte's husband. He shook his head, what an idiot he'd been. He had it on a plate. She wasn't bad looking either. At least she wasn't fake like Libby or Sonja, the pro's wife. He shuddered at the thought of all the silicone and Botox those two had between them.

With funds depleting fast he had to come up with a contingency plan. Libby, he thought, must have settled on a reasonable sum from Bruce. He would be on a decent salary. Perhaps he should visit Libby with an olive branch? Could he go through her tantrums and histrionics again? Depends on how much she's worth once her divorce goes through. Worth a try, he thought. He'd have to bump into her coincidentally though. He'd make a plan.

CHAPTER 8

Charlotte couldn't believe how easily she had got rid of James that morning. She was feeling a little guilty. Perhaps once the absolute arrived, in around six weeks, she'd contact him and check he was ok. Until then she had to keep her distance for her own sanity as well as his. She didn't have a meeting that day. She was actually going to have lunch with her sister and father. Alan had telephoned the day before to arrange to see his daughters. With the new enterprise going on he had hardly seen his girls. He pointed out that all work and no play made George and Charlie dull boys. Her mother would have been turning in her grave on hearing that conversation. She could hear her as if it was only yesterday. "Alan, they are beautiful young girls. No matter how many times you call them boys it is no longer funny. They are of an age where it will start to affect them. I will blame you if they start wearing dungarees and chewing tobacco."

Charlotte and Georgina used to laugh when they heard their parents squabble. It didn't happen often, but when it did both Alan and India would end up laughing together. Charlotte would give anything to have a relationship with a man like her parents had with each other. So lunch was in their favourite bistro in town.

Georgina had arrived first and was sat at the table checking her phone.

"Hello darling, I thought this was going to be a 'no phone zone' today." Charlotte had caught her in the act. She kissed her sister on the cheek and sat down.

"Sorry, I was just about to put it away before Daddy arrived and saw a flagged email. It was from Tom and he never flags emails so I realised it must be urgent." She read through it and sighed. "Bruce has just telephoned him and they're meeting for lunch."

"That isn't unusual." Charlotte was losing interest. She needed a glass of Prosecco. She signalled the waitress. "A glass of Prosecco please, and for you Georgie?" Georgina nodded but didn't lift her head up from Tom's message.

"Oh my God Charlie, Libby is pregnant!" Charlotte quickly did the maths in her head. If the baby was anything under twelve weeks Bruce was off the hook.

"It has to be James's. Does he know?" What complete idiots, it is the twenty-first century, no need for any accidents these days. But the more she thought about it the more she believed that Libby had probably planned it. Her way of making sure she got her hands on James's money. How ironic that she found out too late that he didn't have any.

"Tom says Bruce is in a state of shock as she hasn't told

him how far along she is so it could be his. Surely if it was his she'd be showing big time by now?"

Charlotte agreed. Their Prosecco arrived shortly, followed by their father.

He was filled in with events and for once, with the decree nisi in Charlotte's handbag, Alan could sit and enjoy his daughters company without worrying about them.

By coffee, George was itching to go and see how Tom got on with his lunch with Bruce. Charlotte was equally on tenterhooks and wanted to phone Bruce to reassure him that all would work out fine, just as soon as they could find out how far along Libby was in her pregnancy. Luckily Alan wanted to get home, England were playing Ireland in the Six Nations Cup, kick-off at 3.00 p.m. Tom was due to join him with some beers, but he won't be disappointed if he was a no-show. Sounded like Bruce needed him and Alan knew he was quite capable of turning on the television and pouring himself a beer.

Charlotte followed Georgina to her house, where Tom and Bruce were waiting for the girls, after their pub lunch. Tom had just poured a beer for Bruce and himself. They were discussing the rugby when the girls walked in.

"Hello sweetheart. Not sure I'm going to make it round to your father's this afternoon." It was immediately obvious to George that her husband had been enjoying a few beers with Bruce.

"Don't worry about that. Daddy knows and is fine about it. Are you ok Bruce?" George went over and kissed Bruce on the cheek. Bruce looked like a schoolboy who'd kicked a ball through a window.

"Ah dinnae ken, pet." Whenever Bruce was ruffled he reverted to his native tongue. Charlotte had goosepimples; she loved his Scottish lilt. She decided to take control.

"Bruce." He turned to face her. She had his attention. "Do you ken how far along Libby is?" She thought using a little of his native tongue could help him. To their astonishment he burst out laughing. Tom was laughing too.

"Oh Charlotte, very good effort. You are a breath of fresh air in a bad situation. And to answer your question, I don't know, she wouldn't tell me. She was so busy having hysterics on the phone that I didn't really get any sense out of her except that she was pregnant." Charlotte sighed and shook her head. She remembered the venom that came out of Libby's mouth when she accused her of her underhand tactic of pregnancy to get James back. It looked to Charlotte like Libby had taken the idea one step further.

"Well the only sensible thing to do is to confront her. If she is more than twelve weeks pregnant it hopefully will show. Especially with the type of clothes she normally wears." Annoyingly skin-tight thought Charlotte, but didn't say it aloud. It would sound like jealousy, which it was not. Charlotte could wear skin-tight clothes, she just wouldn't. She suddenly smiled. Nor would Libby if she was pregnant!

"I really don't think I can approach her in the mood she's in. She'd have my slippers out and my dinner warmed, opened and on a plate in no time." They were all laughing. It was quite funny, but they all needed to let their emotions relax. It worked too.

"Well perhaps I should telephone James. He didn't say anything about it this morning when I spoke to him." George looked at her puzzled. "I didn't see the point of telling you he'd called. He was only asking if I was ok because we'd got the decree nisi through today. Anyway, I could see if he knows yet?" She looked at Bruce. He nodded.

"I've got a better idea. I'll ring him." George wasn't sure if that was the beer talking or whether Tom was protecting Charlotte. Whatever it was he was her hero. She reached up and kissed him full on the lips.

"Get a room you two." Bruce was keeping the light-hearted banter going, hoping by the end of the day he was not going to be a father to Libby's baby. He knew that if the baby was his he would love it and care for it for the rest of eternity, but he could think of many other women he'd rather have as his baby's mother than Libby. "Thanks Tom, that sounds like a good idea to me."

Tom left the kitchen to talk to James in private. He wouldn't be able to concentrate with all of them looking at him.

"Hi James, it's Tom. How are things going?" James wasn't surprised to hear from someone in that camp. He'd got off the phone to Libby only twenty minutes earlier. He was in a very bad place. He wanted to get back with Libby, under his terms, but not under duress.

"I take it you've heard from Libby?" James saw no point in polite conversation.

"As a matter of fact, we have." He was about to ask what James had gleaned from his conversation with Libby when James carried on.

"She's up the duff and she says it could be mine. I told her I'd need a DNA test before I believed her. She wasn't happy about that and slammed the phone down on me. I've heard no more since. So you now know as much as I do.

Goodbye Tom." He'd ended the conversation. Tom thought how rude, then remembered he'd been talking to James – par for the course.

Tom went back into the kitchen and related his rather terse conversation with James to them all.

"Who's going to volunteer to talk to Libby? I've done my bit." Tom knew they wouldn't expect him to ring Libby, he felt safe bringing up the obvious next step.

"I suppose I'll have to go and see her. I'm certainly not looking forward to that though." He looked at Charlotte. He couldn't possibly ask her to go with him. He was too much of a gentleman to expect her to suffer the histrionics of his ex-wife, especially after what Libby had done to her. But to his surprise Charlotte read his thoughts.

"I will go with you Bruce, for moral support. Best to go now before she has any more time to think about it and perhaps do something stupid." Charlotte was thinking that Libby was too selfish to think of the little person growing inside her. She'd probably already downed enough alcohol to sink the navy. "I'll drive." He and Tom had managed to get through a pack of beer, not including what they had already drunk at the pub. She picked up her handbag and keys and kissed her sister and brother-in-law and waited by the door for Bruce.

"I think I'm going to see my ex-wife. Thanks for the chat and the beers Tom." They looked at each other. No more need be said. Apart from good luck, but Tom thought better of it. Bruce looked petrified enough.

"You are very brave Charlie, be careful. Come straight back here when you're done. If you're not back in one hour I shall call the emergency services." Georgina was smiling on the outside. She was trying to make light of it for Bruce's sake, seeing the same expression on him as Tom had.

"Don't be daft. We can handle Libby, can't we Bruce? She is just a pussycat at heart." She left laughing out loud. Bruce couldn't help himself and joined in, thankful to Charlotte for being there.

As they drove to Bruce's old home Charlotte wondered how far along their divorce had got. She hadn't asked Bruce about it for a while. She felt it none of her business, but hoped he'd bring up the subject himself. She needed to know before she saw Libby, so she didn't put her foot in it, or make matters worse by saying something out of turn.

"So, have you and Libby finalised your separation yet?" She hadn't time to beat around the bush, as they were about five minutes from their destination.

"I wish. She's not happy with the settlement I was giving her, which was half the house and quarter of my assets. Bearing in mind I was the innocent party here. But she wants the house plus half my assets and wages for the rest of her life, or up to such time as she remarries. I've pointed out that we have no children and she is quite capable of getting a job. My solicitor is trying to make her demands more reasonable but her solicitor is fighting it. It's money for old rope for the solicitors." He sighed. She wanted to put her arms around him and give him a big hug. Luckily, she had to hold the steering wheel.

"Well I think you are being very unreasonable." Bruce looked up at her, puzzled. "How on earth can she get a job that wouldn't break her nails?" They both burst out laughing just as they pulled up to the house. It put everything into perspective. This was just another of Libby's predicaments that had to be overcome. Bruce was used to them so they should be getting easier, although this one was a whammy. They both walked up to Libby's front door. Bruce rang the bell. He pulled up the letterbox and could hear Libby's wailing. She was giving someone a right ear-bashing. Charlotte could hear her from where she was standing. The last sentence resonated out of the letterbox. *"Go to hell James."*

She opened the front door.

"Come to gloat?" She sniffed and walked into her kitchen. Bruce and Charlotte followed her. "Bloody man. How did you put up with him for so long Charlotte?" She spun round to face Bruce. "You can take that petrified look off your face Bruce. You are not the father. Before you ask..." She could see Charlotte looking for evidence around her stomach area. "I'm eight weeks along. My last period was over two months ago." She started wailing again. Charlotte put the kettle on while Bruce tried to calm her down.

"So, I take it James wants nothing to do with it?" Bruce was trying to be matter-of-fact, but he was feeling very sorry for Libby. Libby nodded.

"Well this isn't doing you or the baby any good, sit down and I'll make us all a cup of tea and we can help you decide on the next step." Charlotte took control of the situation.

"Why are you being so nice? And after what I did to you too. I have missed you, Charlie." Libby had mistaken Charlotte's kindness for forgiveness. But at least she'd stopped that infernal wailing, thought Charlotte, so she'd go along with it for the moment.

"So have you been to a doctor yet? You need to make sure you are registered for all the prenatal care things." Bruce wasn't too sure what he was talking about, but he'd listened to enough Radio Four *Women's Hour* programmes whilst driving, to know that once the NHS know you are pregnant, it plans your life until the baby is safely born.

Libby swung around and shouted at Bruce.

"Don't tell me you think I'm making this up. Bruce, I'm shocked that you think I could lie like that." Oh ye of little memory, thought Charlotte. She felt sure having sex behind her husband's back for over a year was tantamount to a few fibs. Bruce didn't want Libby caterwauling again so calmed her down.

"Of course I don't think you are making your pregnancy up. I'm just trying to get you to look after yourself, and the baby." Again, Libby retaliated with words.

"I don't need a doctor. I don't want the baby. If you want to help me you can give me some money to get rid of it." Charlotte shuddered. When did Libby become such a bitch? How could she talk about a little baby growing inside her as if it were a piece of junk that someone needed to take away? Charlotte had to restrain herself from flying at her ex best friend. It took all her self-control to keep her position by the kettle and breathe, slowly. Bruce looked at Charlotte and was worried. He knew it had affected her badly when she had her miscarriage. He had to try to reason with Libby.

"You are not thinking straight, Lib. It's probably your hormones making you say things you don't mean. You need to take your time to work out the best thing for you to do. You also need to sit down calmly with James and..." Before he could finish his sentence, Libby threw herself at Bruce. She was punching him and crying at the same time. Bruce managed to get hold of Libby's wrists and stop the very feeble punches that were raining down on him. He stood up and held her close while she calmed down and stopped crying. In that moment, he realised that he felt very sorry for Libby, but he had no love left for her. He spun her round gently and sat her on the stool he had just vacated. "Right, the first thing we do is get you an appointment with your doctor. You can discuss all your options with him. If you still want to abort this pregnancy after that then he will be able to advise you on all your options. I will cover the costs if need be, after all it'll be coming out of your alimony." He'd tried to make a joke, but Libby wasn't in the mood. Charlotte smiled at him in encouragement. She knew exactly what Bruce was doing. "Shall I phone Dr Saunders for you?" Libby nodded.

Bruce went into the hall to ring the doctor while Charlotte gave Libby a cup of tea. How the mighty fall, she thought. What was it her mother used to say? *"Metis quod seminas"*, you reap what you sow. No truer word had ever been spoken. James had sowed his seed but Libby was definitely not reaping the benefit. Bruce came back in before Charlotte had had to say a word to Libby.

"He said to bring you down now and he can do a pregnancy test and give you a quick check-up. He mentioned blood pressure and something else to do with blood." Charlotte helped him out.

"Could it have been a blood test? They like to check iron levels." Bruce nodded.

"Yes, that was it. Come on Libby, let's get you sorted out and at least healthy so you can make up your mind about the wee bairn." Charlotte led the way out to the car and waited for Bruce to lock up and escort Libby down the driveway. Libby didn't deserve Bruce's help, but Charlotte would expect nothing less from such a kind man.

There was little conversation between them on the way to the doctor's surgery, fortunately only in the next road. Charlotte decided to stay in the car, where she could telephone her sister to keep her abreast of what was going on. Bruce sat in the waiting room with Libby. When her name was called she grabbed his hand.

"No Libby. I'm afraid you have to do this bit by yourself." He felt very hard, but he could not be with her throughout this pregnancy so put his foot down at the beginning. This was not his problem; he had a life of his own and had to keep them separate. He did not want her to rely on him like she could in the past. Those days were well and truly over. He had to make sure she remembered that.

After about fifteen minutes she came back out into the waiting room. She was holding what appeared to be a prescription form. She walked straight out of the door into the carpark. Bruce hurried out after her. Charlotte saw them both in the rear-view mirror. Libby was crying, again. Bruce was holding her, again. Charlotte wondered if she should get out or stay where she was, until she noticed Bruce was guiding Libby towards the car and he was holding her. Charlotte got out and opened the back door where Bruce managed to manoeuvre Libby round, holding her head down and place her on the seat. He shut the door, high-fived Charlotte and got in the front passenger seat. Charlotte smiled to herself. No matter what Libby thinks, Bruce is just being kind, his feelings have been hurt beyond repair where she is concerned. Charlotte got into the driver's side and turned on the engine. She mouthed "Where to?" to

Bruce. He shrugged his shoulders.

"Ok Libby, do you want to get your prescription filled at the chemist before we take you home?" Bruce asked her as he turned towards the back seat.

"No, please can you just take me home." She sounded defeated. They drove on towards her house. "By the way, I'm not pregnant. Just so you know. You can have a good laugh about this later." She started crying.

"Well perhaps it's for the best. Wrong time and all that." Bruce was trying to buck her up, but it wasn't working. Charlotte couldn't understand why Libby was crying when she didn't want a baby anyway. Libby continued.

"Apparently Dr Saunders thinks I have secondary amenorrhea." She could tell both of them hadn't a clue what it was. "It means my periods have stopped, temporarily. He thinks it's due to stress and the fact that I've been on a diet and my body fat index has dropped too low." Both Bruce and Charlotte breathed a silent sigh of relief. No matter what Libby had done, they didn't want her to be ill. "He also thinks I'm depressed and has given me a prescription for antidepressants, which I do not need. I just need to turn the clock back a year. I miss you so much Bruce." She was not wailing, just whimpering, like a child who wanted another sweetie but didn't want to make her mummy cross by crying. She was good, thought Charlotte, but she could tell by Bruce's expression that it wasn't having any impact. Bruce didn't say a word. Charlotte pulled up outside the house and left Bruce to get Libby out and walk her to her door. Not that she expected any different, but Charlotte didn't even get a 'thank you' or a 'goodbye' from her former best friend. Rude.

Bruce came back to the car leaving Libby standing with her front door open but not leaving the doorstep.

"Just drive away." He looked tired. A little sad too Charlotte noticed. "I don't love her any more, I can admit that now, but I do feel responsible for her. Poor wee lass." Charlotte took her hand off the wheel and squeezed Bruce's hand. He looked up at her.

"You are too kind, Bruce Gordon." He smiled. Glad for the fact that such a magnificent woman had his back.

CHAPTER 9

A few weeks after the pregnancy scare, Libby was feeling back to normal. She had taken the doctor's advice and the antidepressants had done the trick. That and the eating properly had brought back her cycle and she felt strong again. She couldn't believe she could ever have felt so miserable. She hadn't cried that much since... ever. No one had called her. She had sent a brusque text message to James telling him she wasn't pregnant, but had heard nothing back. She was glad in a way. He had been worse than useless when she first told him, not like Bruce. She kept thinking the same thing; whatever had she seen in James? Why had she ruined a perfectly good marriage for such a bastard? Could she get Bruce back? She knew in her heart that it was a resounding 'No'. Did she want James back? Not really. What was left? Someone new perhaps, she wondered? She'd heard about online dating and had seen an article in a magazine at the hairdressers. Perhaps she could give that a go. With the prospect of living the rest of her life alone, she made the decision to try it.

She used her maiden name, Libby Bennett-Palmer to sign in, but her profile name was only Libby. She thought it would attract a better class of gentleman. Marital status, she'd have to lie. The divorce was going through but hadn't been finalised.

Hobbies: Can one class beauty as a hobby? Her nails alone took up to an hour a day. She was sure stamp collectors didn't take that long on sticking a few stamps into a book.

Interests: 'Good restaurants', 'good wine', 'holidays abroad' and 'jewellery'. She couldn't think of any other interests but would go back to that one.

Sport: Are either Pilates or yoga a sport? She'd go back to that one too.

Describe yourself: Can she say beautiful? Perhaps that was being a little conceited. She'd settle with *'I take good care of my appearance'*. *'I like good food,'* but she couldn't cook, so added '*cooked for me*'. She was getting into the spirit of online dating. If she was honest, she was rather enjoying talking about herself.

She filled in the personal information about her age, height, eye colour, hair colour and length and body type *'slender'*. Then she came to the tricky questions about religion, education, personality, children, smoking habits, and even piercings and tattoos. They had to be answered with a lot of '*I'd rather not say*' and '*Let's see what happens*' and a few *'absolutely nots'*.

The lifestyle questions made her think. If she told the

truth she would sound boring and bordering on being narcissistic, so she started answering them as if she was Charlotte. As she went through the form she realised how much she missed her best friend. Charlotte's music taste was soul and jazz, Alicia Keys being at the top of her CD collection; she wrote *'Soul, particularly Alicia Keys'*. Libby didn't have a particular genre but liked listening to Charlotte's choices. Films? She couldn't even remember the last film she had watched. Charlotte liked old classics with Cary Grant, James Stewart and Audrey Hepburn and so on. She thought hard and remembered one her mother loved that would make her sound knowledgeable, 'Breakfast at Tiffany's *is one of my classic favourites.'* She made a mental note to make sure she watched it.

She was getting bored. If they didn't have enough information to form an opinion about her (or Charlotte in actual fact!) then they were imbeciles.

Last part was a photograph. That was easy to find as she regarded herself as rather photogenic. She downloaded a rather nice one of herself with a glass of champagne in one hand and a caviar-covered blini in the other. She wistfully remembered the occasion. It was probably the last event where she had been happy. It was the previous New Year's Eve, at Charlotte and James's, before she started the misconceived idea of an affair.

She read through the form in case she had missed anything, pleased with her responses she pressed 'join'. She was immediately forwarded onto the site and could see all the men that the computer thought had things in common with her. She started reading a few profiles of men that looked remotely attractive, ignoring any in tracksuits or vests. That whittled the number down impressively. She then checked out their ages and marital status. Then she discarded any with children. They were just a drain on finances and extra baggage she could do without. She was finally down to a select few. Next she read a few personal statements. The first one tickled her.

"I have two loves in my life, my little rescue Staffie called Oscar and my hamster, Horace." That can't be real. She read another.

"Harley rider, looking for a passenger for days out on the bike." She was beginning to think this was a waste of time. She persevered. Next.

"My mum says I'm good looking and very tidy. She'll be sad to see me move out." She checked the age, forty years old. What a loser, she thought. She realised that she was laughing for the first time in ages. What amazing therapy internet dating was! Next.

"Got to be a Spurs fan." She had a vision of a cowboy on a horse, then realised he meant the football team. She couldn't see very well, tears of laughter were streaming down her cheeks. Next.

"Frog seeks princess with poor eyesight." The next one made her screw up her face. Under hobbies it read *"Camping."* No point in reading any more of that person's info. What self-respecting woman would think camping was a selling point? Do they have electricity in a tent? Where would she plug in her hair dryer? She shook her head in abhorrence. Next one.

"I'm looking for Miss Right and her first name had better not be 'always'!" Sense of humour, albeit warped. She read on.

"I want to ruin your lipstick, not your mascara". She couldn't read any more. Her stomach had started to hurt with her laughing.

Those quotes had to be from Valentine cards. She didn't believe in Valentine's Day – commercial rip-off.

She decided that perhaps that was not the way to go. It had cheered her up, but she was no further forward with her life. She'd check it out again later with a glass of wine and an open mind. For now, she'd go and make herself a coffee and file her nails. They were an annoying length for the keyboard.

James was feeling bad about the way he had left things with Libby. He felt he had closed the door on that relationship; he had wanted to leave it ajar. He was lonely and needed a woman. He toyed with the idea of online dating, but couldn't be bothered going through all that just to end up with a quick one-nighter, even though it would be free. Charlotte was a lost cause. No, he thought, better the devil you know. He'd give Libby a ring that evening, when she'd be at her most vulnerable and he'd invite her out for a meal. He felt gratified that he was doing something nice for her and could ultimately lead to something nice for him in the process.

Charlotte and Bruce had been entertaining Georgina and Tom at the new fish restaurant overlooking the bay called Ocean View Café. The food was good, they all agreed, but they were glad that they were not in any hurry. The waiters were slow to the point of hibernation.

"I'm not going to judge them until we give it a second try in a month's time. Hopefully they'll have got their act together by then." Bruce was helping the ladies into a taxi.

They were going to drop Georgina and Tom home on their way back to Charlotte's. Having drunk more than they had anticipated Bruce and Tom both decided to leave their cars in the restaurant carpark. Tom said he'd pick up Bruce in the morning from Charlotte's. Bruce was offered her spare room, which was getting to be a habit. They both enjoyed each other's company.

"It's early days, but I think they were in too much of a hurry to open to the public. Preparation and planning are so important in a new venture. The problem they will have now is that people will remember their first visit and not want to come again." Charlotte was sad, as the food was amazing. Bruce smiled at her. "What is that look for?" Charlotte loved Bruce's smile.

"Always the businesswoman. That's why your ideas work, preparation and planning rule the day."

"Are you taking the Mickey, Bruce Gordon?" Georgina and Tom were enjoying the entertainment. George was glad to see her sister so happy.

"Och nae hen. I widnae do that to my boss!" Charlotte was laughing. Bruce lapsed into his native tongue the more drunk he got.

By the time they had dropped her sister and brother-in-law off and got home it was very late. Bruce had popped into the kitchen and was warming some milk up for a night-time cocoa. Charlotte loved the routine they had both got into when Bruce stayed. They were like a married couple without the benefits. Did she just think that? She remonstrated with herself in her mind. What they had was true friendship, any further and it could ruin it all. She went into the kitchen where Bruce was pouring the milk into two mugs. He put the saucepan into the sink and ran cold water into it. Was it the drink, or was she watching his every move with impropriety in her thoughts. Bruce snapped her out of it.

"Come on, ye look tired, lassie, off to bed. I'll lock up and put the cat out." She took the mug from him and then looked up at his smiling face.

"I haven't got a cat." He laughed at her puzzled gaze.

"It's a saying my Aunty Hennie used to use, meaning it was time for bed and all visitors had to go home." He locked the kitchen door and checked the front door as he passed it. Charlotte was halfway up the stairs. She turned round and watched him turn the lights off. She felt totally secure and happy when Bruce was around. She made her way to her room and placed the mug on her bedside table. Bruce put his head round her door. "Sleep tight, don't let the bed bugs bite." He winked at her.

"You sleep well too." He was about to turn when she called him back. "Bruce?"

"Aye." He hovered meaning to go but wanting to eek it out as long as he could.

"Thank you for being such a good friend. I don't know how I would have coped without you." She moved to her bedroom door and kissed him on the cheek.

"My pleasure. Night night." He turned and left to go to Charlotte's spare room. It had taken every ounce of willpower not to have grabbed her and whisked her onto the bed and kissed her full on the lips. He was falling for her but didn't want to ruin her trust in him.

Charlotte settled down under her duvet, thinking thoughts that she could not believe. How funny life was. Bruce had been a wonderful friend for a long time but now she was seeing him in a very different light. She imagined herself going down to breakfast and he was making his renowned Scottish pancakes. He turned to see her in the doorway and opened his arms for her to enter into the most beautiful embrace. His lips glided onto hers and it felt more passionate than she could ever remember feeling with anyone else, ever.

"*BANG...*" She was startled out of her reverie by a loud noise outside her window. It sounded like the wind had blown the wheelie bin over, but it wasn't windy. Grudgingly she got out of her warm bed, postponing her ultimate dream of the decade, and went over to her window to check what had just happened.

"*Shit.*" James realised he'd woken her up. He was trying to climb into the lounge through one of the fanlight windows. The middle one had a loose catch and he was sure it would have been the furthest thing on her mind to have had it fixed. He was right, but unfortunately due to the height he had 'borrowed' the blue wheelie bin and it had not been very steady, placed on the uneven paving slabs. He looked up at her window, only to see her very angry face, with the help of the street lighting, looking down at him.

She wanted to laugh; James looked so pitiful lying on the grass with the recycling bin on its side on the path. Unfortunately, the full picture suddenly dawned on her and she wanted to shout at him to go away and never come back. Charlotte was just lifting the catch of her window to tell James to go away when a blue haze enveloped her whole consciousness. It took her a moment, but then she realised that the blueness was from a police car's flashing lights. She pushed the window catch back into the locked position and walked across her bedroom grabbing her dressing gown off the back of her door, she went onto the landing where Bruce was already waiting for her.

"He's a pain in the arse that ex of yours!" He was smiling and something told her that the police hadn't come past by chance. He put his arm around her and held her tightly. He could see the blood had drained from her face.

"How did you know he was here?" Her voice sounded muffled but she didn't want to pull away from the security of his embrace.

"Well, I didn't want to worry you earlier, but I saw his car parked on the corner as our taxi pulled up outside here. If I had told you, you wouldn't have slept at all. I have been keeping an eye on his movements and had to time the phone call from his attempted illegal entry. Luckily his first attempt at the back door didn't work as I had bolted it. That was when I dialled 999 and reported an attempted break-in. I thought they'd miss him, but he played right into our hands by having another attempt via the lounge window." How long had she been dreaming? A lot seemed to have happened while she thought she was awake. Thank goodness Bruce had stayed the night. He gently let go of her and went down to talk to the police officer that was tapping at the front door.

Bruce was still dressed and went outside with the officer. James was in the back of the police car looking very sorry for himself. Bruce explained the circumstances, and the police officer took a few notes.

"Unfortunately, this is a civil violation. We can only arrest him if it was a criminal act. You need to get Mrs Whitfield to go to court and get an injunction to stop the pestering. Then we can arrest him if he is in breach of a court order. Sorry, but that's all we can do. We can take him in and tell him off, but I'm not sure that will help by the sound of it. We will let him go and we'll stay around the area for a while to check he doesn't come back tonight." The officer looked empathetic but his hands were tied.

Bruce thanked him and went back inside to talk to Charlotte. He had to persuade her to go to her solicitors in the morning to set something more cogent in motion. He didn't think it would take much persuasion.

He went back inside and found Charlotte up on a chair at the lounge fanlight window.

"This latch is broken. He must have known." Bruce took hold of her hand and steered her down off the chair. He took a look at the catch and wiggled it.

"If you have a Philips screwdriver handy, I can fix it now for you." She ran into the kitchen and rifled through her drawers. Bruce watched the police take James out of the car and escort him over to his own, which was out of his sight. The officers came back shortly afterwards, but Charlotte had missed it all.

"Found one. It's a bit rusty I'm afraid." She handed it up to Bruce.

"That'll do nicely. It just needs tightening up. There, all better." He turned and smiled at her. "Looking at the size of this window I don't think even a Dickensian orphan would have got through this without a struggle." He wanted to reassure Charlotte that she was safe. "We'll go to the solicitor together tomorrow. Then I'll take you out for lunch. Work can wait for one morning." He winked at her. "My boss is very understanding." Charlotte laughed. Bruce got down and took the chair back into the kitchen from where Charlotte had carried it. "Now, I don't know about you, but I need my beauty sleep." He took hold of her hand and they walked back upstairs. He stopped outside her bedroom door and kissed her on the cheek. "Goodnight Charlotte. You can sleep well now. He won't be stupid enough to come back tonight." He let go of her hand and gave her a gentle nudge into her room. She turned round and looked at him.

"I'm not sure I will be able to sleep. I'm half expecting a brick through my window." She was shivering. It wasn't the cold, Bruce realised, clearly she was really scared. He didn't blame her either after all she had been through.

"Would you like me to stay with you for a while?" He didn't want her to get the wrong idea, but she needed the company. "I'll lie on your bed next to you until I hear you snoring!" Charlotte laughed again. He was such good therapy.

With her snuggled under her quilt Bruce did as he said and plonked himself unceremoniously on the top, fully dressed. He would have liked to snuggle under the duvet with her, but he did not want to take advantage of her vulnerability at that moment. Hopefully when all the chaos of the two divorces had been resolved and they were both free agents he could perhaps tell Charlotte how he felt about her, but until then, hard as it may be, it was safer and more chivalrous to keep the bond between them as genuine straightforward friendship. He crept out of her room some twenty minutes later, after hearing her breathing change and her grip on his hand relax. Before he went to bed he took one quick inspection of the grounds and the road. When he was satisfied he'd seen nothing untoward he took himself off to bed.

Bruce was already downstairs with breakfast in full swing when Charlotte surfaced.

"Was I dreaming or did that really happen last night?" Charlotte wandered over to the cooker and smelt the delicious pancakes browning nicely on the griddle.

"I'm afraid so. You need to phone the solicitors." Bruce moved her gently towards the breakfast table and sat her down.

"I don't think anyone will be there yet. I'll wait until nine o'clock. Thank you for last night Bruce. You are my hero." She smiled up at him as he leant over with a plate of pancakes.

"You're welcome. Now eat these before they get cold. Strawberry jam or syrup?" She loved both.

"Which are you having?" Bruce looked like a naughty child.

"Both!" Charlotte agreed that would be the solution to her dilemma too.

They continued breakfast chatting about the business, the breakfast and the day ahead. Charlotte realised that was what had been missing from her life. She also realised she hadn't had conversations over breakfast for a very long time. How did she not notice her life changing so dramatically? She wondered if she had been in denial all that time. Had she been too busy to notice? She won't let that happen again. She was enjoying Bruce's company more than she thought possible after James's betrayal. But Bruce had restored her faith in men, well at least established her ultimate faith in Bruce.

CHAPTER 10

Jeremy calmed Charlotte down and explained the next step to keep James away from troubling her. It was all in a days work for him. He normally gave civil action cases to his associate, but Charlotte trusted him.

"Right. We'll get an injunction rolling. At least then the police can arrest him on the spot if he pesters you again. Now the only thing that worries me is the money you are paying him by direct debit. Do you want it stopped?" Charlotte hadn't thought about it. If she stopped the money things would only get worse.

"Let's see how he behaves once he has been issued with the injunction. If he keeps out of my life he can keep receiving the money. There can't be many payments left anyway. I only promised six months' rent." She'd check with her bank when she got home. Unfortunately James was on a downward spiral and it didn't look like he'd be earning his own rent for a while yet. But that wasn't her problem, she kept telling herself. "Thank you Jeremy for all your help. Let's hope the status quo is restored before I lose my mind and business."

"I'm sure that won't happen. From what I can see of your new venture, you are onto another winner. I hope I can get rid of this obstacle for you so you can enjoy the fruits of your labour." He shook her hand as she got up. "I'll keep in touch and let you know when it's safe for you to go out again." He was smiling. She knew it was his attempt at humour. What she didn't know was the extent of his anxiety. He'd do all he could to prevent her any more stress. But would that be enough?

"Jeremy, you are an angel and thank you for seeing me at such short notice especially for something as trivial as my ex-husband's schoolboy behaviour. Let's hope we've nipped it in the bud." She left his room feeling a little stronger, after all the law was on her side. She just hoped James would adhere to it.

Bruce was waiting in the car for her. He thought it would only complicate things if he'd gone into the solicitors with Charlotte. People could be very judgemental. It was a shame that friendship and loyalty could be misread with ulterior motives and sordid innuendos. Such were folk with little minds, thought Bruce. He was still tutting to himself when Charlotte came out of the front door into the carpark. Bruce got out and opened the passenger door for her.

"Well, thank you, kind sir." She was smiling at him. It was as if a weight had been lifted from her shoulders. The sympathy she had misplaced on James had well and truly run its course and she had a happier, healthier attitude of anger towards him now. "Let's keep your boss waiting a little longer and spoil ourselves at the pub!" Bruce didn't need to be told twice. He shut her door and almost skipped round to the other side. Her cheerfulness was catching. He also realised that it was the first time in a while that she had a grin on her face. Little did James know that he had done them both a favour; Charlotte needed closure and James had given it to her.

James woke with a headache and an awful feeling he'd done something the night before that caused a problem, but couldn't remember what. He stretched over the bed to reach his watch. It was 11.45 a.m. He had a meeting with some new clients from an export company at noon. Unless he wanted them to see an image of a drunk, unemployed loser, he was going to have to telephone them and postpone the appointment. He grabbed his mobile and checked his calendar. Their phone number was there and he tested his voice before he called them. After coughing he retched. His head was over the bed and he managed to pull an old newspaper under him before the contents of his stomach ended up covering a beautiful picture of the Northern Lights from a cruise ship, sailing from Southampton. The headline read,

"Is a Northern Lights Cruise on your bucket list?" James thought just the bucket would have been useful at that moment. How did he let himself get into that state? He remembered getting home and opening a bottle of wine. Where had he been? He banged his head with the palm of his hand and then regretted it. He tried to get off the bed and noticed his knee hurt. He looked down and saw mud on his trousers. Why was he still dressed? He must have had

more than a bottle. He managed to get to the bathroom before another wave of nausea caught hold of him. After stripping off and showering he was feeling more human and images were floating into his mind of blue bins and blue lights.

"Oh, fricking hell!" It was all coming back to him in glorious technicolour. He had a vision of Charlotte looking down on him with disdain and disgust. "What the hell have I done?" he said aloud, as if someone was going to answer the question for him. He remembered getting very angry when he saw a picture on Instagram of Charlotte and Bruce with Tom and Georgina at the new fish restaurant he himself had wanted to try. Tom had forgotten to block him. He had blocked him from his Facebook page, but for some reason he had forgotten Instagram, probably because he used it less. James remembered going round to his old house thinking he could get in and wait for Charlotte to return. Surprise was the element he needed. She would have no control of the situation and he'd have the upper hand, for once. Then he'd tell her straight that he was going to move back in and they were going to live happily ever after, or something like that.

He had pulled up on the corner to make sure there were no other cars in the driveway. Then it dawned on him that she may invite them all back for a drink. He'd sat and waited for her return. He saw the taxi pull up. Good sign, he thought. Hopefully she was a little inebriated. He couldn't see the front of the house from where he was, but thought if he gave her around half an hour she would hopefully be in bed by then. His idea was to use the key he left hidden in the shed for emergencies hoping the lock hadn't been changed. If it had he'd go to Plan B, the lounge fanlight window that he had meant to fix.

He remembered slinking up the driveway like a burglar, checking to see if the bedroom light was out. He used his phone's torch to find the key in the shed. Having found it he tried it in the back door. Annoyed when he realised the door had been bolted from inside. Charlotte had never bothered doing that before. Someone had been putting ideas in her head about security. He guessed probably the Scottish prick. He had then gone round to the front of the house and realised he would not reach the small fanlight without a lift. Looking around he'd seen the blue recycling bin. That would do nicely he thought...

"Oh shit." He didn't want to remember the rest. What an idiot. He'd blown any chance of reconciliation by those antics. His head was throbbing like mad. He'd forgotten to phone the new clients. He'd send them an email with an excuse about a death in the family or something. Perhaps he could phone Charlotte too and tell her he didn't know what he was doing as he'd been drinking and wondered why he couldn't get into his house. If he made out he'd forgotten they were no longer together she may take pity on him. She may find it amusing. He thought not. The problem would be that the police had let him drive away. They would have checked him and known he was stone cold sober before letting him take charge of a vehicle. He'd have to think of another tack. He'd played Mr Nice Guy for long enough. The bitch needed bringing down a peg or two. He had to think of a plan that would make her listen and be open to an amicable resolution that would mean they could be together again, with him working for her and paying him what he deserved, in the comfort of his own home. He'd get rid of that Scottish jackoff, or jockoff more appropriately.

"Ha ha ha!" He laughed at his own joke. Hopefully Bruce will go back to the luscious Libby, the Barbie doll. The more he thought about Libby, the angrier he got. Again the same phrase played around in his grey matter. "What a bloody idiot I've been."

Bruce had dropped Charlotte off at her house after their pub lunch. He had to go to the bank and then to his flat to check everything was ok there. He wouldn't put anything past James in the frame of mind he was in at that time. Jeremy had left a message for Charlotte on her answer machine to say he'd managed to get evidence from the officer who had attended the incident the night before, and who had luckily been on duty that afternoon so an interim application had been made to the court and he would let her know if she was needed to appear if it was granted. Having looked up the injunction process she knew what it meant, and was glad she didn't have to face James; at least not until he'd been served notice. For her own peace of mind, she hoped sooner rather than later.

"Hello, anyone home?" Charlotte smiled and went to the back door. Her father was standing holding a bunch of flowers. "Hello darling. Thought these might cheer you up." Charlotte got a big hug too.

"Has my sister been telling tales again?" Charlotte had rung Georgina while Bruce was ordering the food at the bar. She played down the night before, but Georgina knew James too well. "Thank you, Daddy, let me put those in water."

"Well, what happened? I got a garbled message about a wheelie bin and the police. For goodness sake, why can't the man grow up and act his age?" Charlotte looked at her father who was shaking his head. He was looking tired. He didn't need the worry. She needed to take control of her life again. She put her arms around her father's neck and told him not to worry, that Jeremy had everything in hand.

"What about a nice cup of tea?" She went to fill the kettle.

"You sound just like your mother. When in doubt put the kettle on for a nice cup of tea." He chuckled. Charlotte smiled at him. Instead of thinking how awful things were, she had so much going for her, an amazing family and a good friend in Bruce, which was more than most and definitely more than James had. She took a deep breath and started to relax and enjoy her father's company. After their cup of tea she asked to be excused to change into more comfortable clothing. She was still in her formal suit for her meeting with Jeremy. The day was too far-gone for her to go out and do any work, so trackies and perhaps a little drink were the order of the day. She felt relaxed and secure with her father there.

Alan started putting the crockery into the dishwasher when the telephone rang.

"Charlie, Charlie..." he shouted up the stairs. He could hear the water running and realised she had opted for a quick shower. He'd take a message for her in case it was important.

"Hello, Charlotte's phone." He couldn't think how else to answer it.

"Hello, is Charlotte there please?" Alan swore he

recognised that polished, Public School voice, but wasn't too sure.

"I'm afraid she's indisposed at the moment. May I take a message, or get her to call you back. This is her father." He just wanted to make sure the caller knew they were talking to someone who actually knew Charlie.

"Oh, hello Alan. It's Jeremy here. Thought I recognised your voice." Jeremy breathed a sigh of relief. He can tell Alan the bad news to pass on to Charlotte.

"I thought it was you, but wasn't sure. How are you Jeremy? Thank you for helping Charlotte, by the way. Weight off my mind with you on her side, I can tell you."

"I'm afraid you won't think that in a minute. Unfortunately, I have just been talking to the Judge appointed to this case. He feels the injunction is overkill at this stage. He would rather go down the 'sit the couple down and talk' scenario. I agreed that the one incident last night was not enough to address the court with, but pointed out that there have been numerous incidents that haven't involved the police. He wants everything from now on noted with evidence, for example screen shots of conversations, photos of him stalking, audio copies of verbal harassment and so on. Sorry Alan for this news, but the judge has the last word on this one." Jeremy sounded defeated. Alan sighed and shook his head. Just when Charlotte was cheering up and getting her life back in order too.

"Let me get this straight. The judge would rather Charlotte waited until she was taken into the intensive care unit or the psychiatric ward before she made a fuss? Honestly Jeremy, I thought protection of women had come further in recent years." Jeremy expected Alan to be protective of his daughter.

"I'm afraid it all boils down to finance. They don't want to 'waste' the courts time on cases they feel an amicable resolution can be attained. It is procedure to be fair to the judge, if there is a lack of evidence. This is why I need you to make Charlotte understand that everything from now on that involves James and his behaviour to her or any member of your family and friends has to be logged and if necessary reported to the police if it is significant."

Alan could hear Charlotte shutting drawers in her room. He needed to compose himself. "OK Jeremy thanks anyway for all you have done so far. I will tell Charlotte and the rest of the family to be vigilant and make sure we all have our phones on camera setting when we go out." He knew it wasn't Jeremy's fault and realised that he was probably making him feel inadequate, which wasn't his intention at all. "I'm glad you are there for Charlotte, Jeremy, I know you are on her side, which you have the whole family's appreciation for. Goodbye for now. We'll keep in touch." Jeremy was glad to end the conversation. He felt he'd let Charlotte and her family down. He'd known them since he was a boy when his father was Alan and India's solicitor. They were a lovely family and didn't deserve the things they had gone through. The one thing on their side, he thought, was that they were a very close family that made them stronger. He had no doubt they would get through the whole contemptible mess hopefully unscathed.

Bruce arrived at the house just before Georgina and Tom. He got out of his car and walked over to theirs.

"You two have been summoned as well then? Any idea what it's about?" George shook her head.

"No. Daddy just called and asked if we could pop over for a family chinwag. Thought it strange at the time, even stranger now you are here too." George waited for Tom to lock their car and walked in with both of them.

Charlotte was sitting in her lounge, on the settee, drinking a large glass of red wine. Her father was sitting opposite her in an armchair with a small glass of something alcoholic. George reckoned it was a small brandy by the look of it.

"Help yourselves to a drink, we may be here for a while." Charlotte got up and hugged her sister. Tom and Bruce kissed her on the cheek. George opened her mouth to speak but Charlotte put her finger up and pointed to the kitchen. George followed the men into the kitchen where they were sorting out the drinks. Once they all had a drink in their hands Charlotte explained exactly what Jeremy had said to her father, with Alan interspersing with points to clarify what he'd heard.

For a while no one talked. Bruce couldn't keep quiet for long.

"I raise my glass in a toast: to the demise of James Whitfield. He should ne're have married for money, ye'll borrow it cheaper!" Bruce had toasted in a broad Scottish accent. It had done the trick. They were all laughing and clinking their glasses to the unique toast. Alan caught Bruce's eye and winked with a smile. Bruce knew exactly what he meant. They both loved Charlotte and Alan was happy Bruce was there unfalteringly in her corner.

CHAPTER 11

James had not had a good day. He'd been discarded by clients, abandoned by his friends and was feeling very sorry for himself. How things had changed for him in the last year. Thinking back to exactly a year ago he would have been at the dining table eating a very enjoyable meal in their lovely home. He'd had an extremely comfortable lifestyle. He looked around at the room he was in, papers everywhere. Dirty washing bulging out of a carrier bag ready for the launderette. There were empty bottles and dirty glasses on a heavily stained coffee table. Basically he was living like a hobo. He wanted his old privileges back. He started humming to himself and realised it was an old Joni Mitchell song, 'Big Yellow Taxi'. He blasted out the chorus hoping it would make him feel better. The sentiment of the song suited his mood. You really don't know what you've got till it's gone.

He stopped singing but continued humming the tune. A plan was already forming in his mind. He'd need all his acting skills he had honed during the last few months of his marriage. He picked up his phone and called Libby. The plan would only work if she picked up.

"Hello James. What do you want?" She didn't sound happy to hear from him, but at least she'd answered.

"Hi Libby. I was worried about you. I haven't heard from you and wanted to make sure you were ok." He had to play it slowly or she'd get suspicious. "I hated the way things had been left. I hope you can forgive me for being an arse." There was silence at the other end. He wondered if she'd put the phone down. He heard her swallow. "If you are not busy I would love to take you out for a meal. No strings. I just want to apologise properly. I can pick you up if you like." Luckily he had his car for a couple more weeks before it would be repossessed. He could almost hear the cogs in Libby's brain turning. Eventually she responded.

"I'll be ready at 7.30, but no strings James, just a meal." Yes, thought James. Stage one complete. It would cost him the price of a meal, but if he could get Libby back with Bruce it would be worth it, leaving the way clear for him to entice Charlotte back into his arms.

"Seven-thirty it is. I shall be there on the dot. Bye Libby, see you later." There was no goodbye from Libby. The phone had gone dead.

Libby couldn't believe she had agreed. But she had to admit an apology from James would mean closure. A meal out would be nice too. She'd have to be on her guard though; James had been very unpredictable of late.

On the dot of seven-thirty, his car drew up outside Libby's house. She went out to meet him so he wouldn't get a chance to enter her home. James got out of the car and opened the passenger door for Libby.

"Your carriage awaits, m'lady." He smiled at her. She noticed the old cheeky James was on form. Perhaps he'd had time to realise how badly he had treated her and genuinely wanted to make amends.

"Thank you, James. It is nice to see you." She got into the car. James walked round to the driver's side and was glad Libby couldn't mind-read. He had forgotten how much he loathed her. During the short distance to the restaurant James had chosen, he decided to test the water.

"Have you heard from Bruce? How is he?" He glanced at Libby who was staring at her fingernails.

"I'd rather not talk about Bruce, James. He has made his feelings towards me abundantly clear. Our divorce is going through without a problem so I will be free of him and Charlotte very soon." She began to sniff. Oh God, thought James, please don't blubber now.

"Do you want to get back with him though?" He asked very softly as if he wanted to help.

"I have betrayed him James. He has been hurt beyond measure. *We* hurt him James. My life is now wrecked. I am soiled goods. I don't want to apportion blame, but I wish you had never kissed me that night." She was remembering the first time James kissed her in his hallway while the others were still at the table having after-dinner drinks. James was trying to keep his temper. He was seething inside. The evening was not going according to plan. The bitch was now crying and blubbing away telling him it was all his fault. He screeched on the brakes. He'd had enough. He got out of the car and went round to her side. She looked out and couldn't understand why he had stopped in the middle of the shady part of town. The only restaurants in that area were take-aways.

"Get out." He said angrily grabbing her arm and almost wrenching her shoulder out of its socket.

"James, what are you doing?" He managed to get her half out of the car and pulled with more effort. She was on the pavement with a nasty gash on her leg from the corner of the car door. She kept very still and quiet. She was petrified.

"I'll tell you what I'm doing. I'm putting you out with the rest of the trash. YOU seduced ME. You whore. You are no better than the streetwalkers on the corner there." He pointed to a couple of girls outside a 24/7 convenience store, scantily clad and obviously looking out for trade.

He left her on the ground and reached into the car glove-compartment. He pulled out a handy pocket size pack of tissues and threw them at her.

"Don't say I'm not considerate." He laughed at his little joke. Walked round to the driver's side and drove off, leaving Libby shivering from fear and despair.

"Are you ok, love?" She looked up and saw the girls from the corner had come over to help her. "Here, let's get you sorted." The older girl was opening the tissue packet and dabbing her leg with one. The younger girl kept an eye on the road. They are obviously still working, thought Libby. It was kind of them to care.

"Thank you for helping me. You are very kind." The older girl smiled at her.

"We have to stick together us girls." She said, and winked. Oh, my goodness, thought Libby, they think I'm a prostitute too. She looked at herself, bedraggled and with a massive hole in her tights. She did look a sight.

"Sharon, we've got a punter." The younger girl was talking to a chap through an open car door window.

"Will you be ok?" The older girl was concerned. Libby didn't want her to miss out on her evening's proceeds so waved her away.

"I'll be fine now, thank you." She got up off the floor the bleeding had subsided for the moment. "Have a good night." She couldn't think of anything else appropriate to say.

"Thanks love, and you." They got into the back of the car together. Safety in numbers, thought Libby.

She was alone, on a street in a dubious neighbourhood. She looked in her bag and realised she hadn't bothered to take her purse with her, thinking James had invited her so she'd not have needed any money. How wrong can a person be about another person? All the alarm bells had rung but she had chosen to ignore them, due to loneliness. She had to get home somehow. She knew she couldn't walk – her leg was very painful. She took her phone out of her bag and called the only person she could trust. There was no answer. She really didn't want to leave a message and so hung up. Who else could she ring? In the old days, she wouldn't even have had to think about it. Sadly, she had no one else but she was desperate, so she called Charlotte.

Charlotte was clearing away the glasses after George and Tom had left. Alan had just said goodbye and Bruce was walking him down the driveway to his car, hopefully putting his mind at rest. Charlotte knew they were ganging up on her, but didn't mind.

Bruce's phone was ringing when she was walking to the kitchen with the dirty nibbles plates. She put the plates on the worktop and went back to the lounge and was about to take the phone out of Bruce's jacket pocket when it rung off. She ignored it. She'd tell Bruce he'd missed a call when he got back. She went back to the kitchen and opened the dishwasher. While putting the glasses and plates in she heard her phone ringing. She dashed back into the lounge and looked on the coffee table at her phone. For the first time in a while she saw Libby's name flash up on the screen. She took a deep breath and answered it. After all, it had to be urgent for Libby to call her. She then realised that Bruce's missed call was probably Libby too.

"Hello." Charlotte didn't mean to sound abrupt, but really didn't want Libby to get into the habit of phoning her when she couldn't get hold of Bruce.

"Hello, Charlie. It's Libby. Sorry to bother you but I'm in a bit of a mess." Charlotte heard the angst in Libby's voice and could tell by her breathing and her voice that she was crying.

"OK Libby, slow down and tell me what's happened." Charlotte needed to calm Libby down if she had any hope of helping her.

"James has dumped me in the street, my leg is bleeding and I've no money." Charlotte needed her to stop crying so she could understand exactly what had happened and where she was.

"Libby, where are you?" Libby was trying to talk. Charlotte could hear her taking deep breaths. She was obviously trying to compose herself. Charlotte tried again. "Libby, where are you?"

"I don't know." She looked around for a landmark that would give her position away. She'd never been to that part of town and had no idea the name of the road. *"There's a 24/7 convenience store on the corner."*

Good grief thought Charlotte. Every corner on every street had a convenience store!

"Libby are there any taxis in the area?" She needed to get her to safety. Charlotte forgot about her acrimony towards her ex-best-friend and needed to get her home.

"But I haven't any money Charlie." Charlotte could hear Libby wailing again.

"Libby don't worry about money. Just get a taxi to bring you to my house and I'll pay the driver when he gets here. Go to the convenience store and ask them to call you a taxi. They will help, I'm sure." Charlotte had her fingers crossed, metaphorically speaking.

"Why are you being so kind to me, I don't deserve it after the way I've treated you." Charlotte had to agree, but that wasn't going to help Libby at that moment. *"I'm outside the convenience store. Hopefully I'll see you soon."* The phone went dead. Charlotte noted that Libby wasn't waiting for an answer to her question. As it happened Charlotte didn't have an answer, except no one would kick a man when he's down, if they'd been brought up properly.

Charlotte could hear the kitchen door close. Bruce was back.

"Well you just missed all the fun." Charlotte explained about the phone call and told him that she had invited Libby back to the house and that they would pay for the taxi.

"Had she not learnt a lesson from this? Why on earth did she go out again with James?" It was beyond him.

"Loneliness I would imagine. Libby has always been a party animal, must have been too much for her to be ostracised from her old life." Bruce nodded in agreement.

"You are a wonderful woman, you know, truly magnanimous. You had every right to tell Libby to find another sucker to help her. Thank you for that. My worry now is that Libby has been prone to exaggeration." Charlotte heard the desperation in Libby's voice, and she was not that good an actor.

"I didn't want to take the risk after James's recent behaviour. Looks like we may have our fodder for the courts quicker than we thought." Bruce looked out of the lounge window. There was a tell-tale sound of a diesel engine.

"Taxi." He grabbed his jacket for his wallet and went outside to pay the driver. Charlotte watched from the window. What she saw shocked her. Bruce was helping Libby up the driveway, limping and bedraggled and looking far from her best with his jacket draped over her shoulders. Charlotte immediately felt sorry for her ex-best-friend. Charlotte the aggrieved was in a far happier place than Libby the perpetrator.

Bruce took Libby to the kitchen and sat her on a stool putting her damaged leg onto another. It looked worse than it was after a thorough clean with disinfectant. As Libby squealed with the sting Bruce felt nothing. She told him exactly what had happened in between sobs. Bruce looked up and saw Charlotte in the doorway behind Libby. He smiled at her. Charlotte knew he wasn't going to fall for Libby's sympathy-seeking tactics. What was it her grandmother used to say? Ah yes, 'You've made your bed, now lie in it.' How apt she thought. She smiled back at

Bruce. Time to confront her ex-best-friend.

"Hello Libby, cup of tea?" She went to fill the kettle, totally distracting Libby from her play for Bruce.

"Oh, yes please Charlie. Thank you for inviting me. I don't know what I would have done if you hadn't answered your phone." Charlotte thought she was being very cynical but was Libby sounding that sincere? Or was she still playing up to Bruce using the sympathy card? Well it obviously wasn't working because Charlotte could read Bruce's body language very well and he wasn't happy.

"You will have to report this incident to the police, Libby." Not wanting to give too much away, or the reasons, Bruce had to make Libby realise it was a good idea. "James has been in a bad place for a while and who knows what he may do next. At least if you have reported him it will be easier for you to get legal help if need be to keep him away." Libby hadn't thought about any of that. It did seem a good idea though.

"I'll report it tomorrow. It's a bit late now. I'm so tired after all that has happened to me." Here she goes again, thought Charlotte. "I didn't get any dinner either." She laughed. Charlotte really didn't want Libby staying for dinner, but she also didn't want Bruce to feel guilty and ending up taking her home to cook for her. Bruce took it out of her hands.

"There is enough here for you to stay for dinner, if that's ok with Charlotte, but as soon as you have finished I'll put you in a taxi so you can get home to bed." Good for you, thought Charlotte. "Neither of us can drive as we're already over the limit." Well that's told her in a nutshell. He caught Charlotte's eye and winked. There was no way Charlotte was going to allow Libby to take another man from her. She was falling for Bruce more and more each day. She hoped the feeling was mutual.

Libby wondered if Bruce was staying the night with Charlotte, but didn't want to know the answer.

CHAPTER 12

By the time James had got home, picking up a pizza on the way, he was seething. Why he thought he could rely on that airhead Libby was beyond him. He had to start thinking outside the box. His best chance of getting Charlotte back was taking Bruce out of the picture. That he had already surmised. He had now come to the conclusion that he had to do it himself.

His first thought was to cut Bruce's brake line. He'd seen it done in films, but do people really do that in real life? Thinking it through realistically, the main flaw in that plan was if Charlotte was in the car at the time. Poison was out as he wouldn't be able to get close enough to administer it. A random shooting wouldn't work, where would he get a gun from for starters? He'd also need to practise for a few years before he could hit a moving target in the right place. Perhaps in New York he could get away with it, but in a town like theirs on the Dorset coast, it would not go unnoticed. He would be the first suspect. He wondered if there was an *Idiots Guide* to murder on Amazon's book list. Perhaps Google could help. He logged in to his computer and in Google search he typed *How to get away with murder*. Immediately he was seeing actors' faces and a link into an American Drama Series, Season 3. Perhaps he ought to watch an episode to get an idea.

He took a big gulp of very cheap wine and stopped to think. He only had a month or two left rent-free. His Mercedes would be repossessed if he didn't make a lease payment soon. His sensible ego knew he could make enough money from his field of knowledge to cover all his debts and be left with plenty to live on. If he could stop his infatuation for his ex-wife and start looking for a new beginning with a new woman, he could make a very comfortable life again for himself. Only his sensible ego could be totally concealed by his obsessive ego to the point of destruction. He knew that and wanted to change. Tomorrow was another day. He would get up, shower, spruce himself up by getting rid of the stubble from his face, dress smartly and get off to the Golf Club to mend some bridges and hopefully get himself some lucrative clients by taking control of his life again. He went to bed feeling calm for the first time in a while.

Bruce and Charlotte were sitting in the lounge having got rid of Libby, without any feeling of guilt. They had both been civil and generous to Libby but they did it from sympathy, not friendship.

"Do you think she'll go to the police station tomorrow?" Charlotte didn't think she would.

"No." Bruce didn't either. "I think she will be too embarrassed. The way James has treated her she had to be so desperate to give him another chance."

"Or stupid." Charlotte felt mean saying that, but she had no sympathy left. Bruce knew that the whole evening must have been a strain on Charlotte, more so than him. He put his arm around her and held her close, in a best friend kind of way. Bruce seemed to stay more often at Charlotte's than his own flat, but still in the spare room. They tended to do most of their work in the evening over a bottle of wine, enjoying each other's company. They had both been through the same emotional roller coaster but were mending very nicely. That night proved that there was no retribution or revenge in his or her minds against Libby. But then they were both in happier mindsets.

Their cosy snuggle was rudely interrupted by Bruce's phone ringing. Charlotte thought it was Libby so got up to leave Bruce to sort her out, whilst she went to the kitchen to boil the milk for their cocoa. She loved the new routine she had fallen into. She stopped at the kitchen door. Bruce was sounding very concerned, his speech had altered to broad Scottish and his voice had gone up a few octaves. Something was wrong and it wasn't Libby. She moved back into the lounge and caught the word 'accident' and then 'infirmary'. She knew that was what the Scottish called their hospitals.

"Och, ok Roderick, I'll caw ye in the mornin. Ay. Bye the noo." Bruce looked up at Charlotte. She was looking very concerned but wondered if it was any of her business, so waiting for him to explain the conversation he had just had.

"That was my cousin Roderick, from Perth. My mother

and aunt have been in a car accident on their way back from shopping. They have been taken to the local infirmary. My Aunt Flora had rung Roderick from the ambulance so he managed to talk to the paramedics. They said they'd probably keep the ladies in overnight because of their age. Unfortunately, my mother heard them and called them cheeky rascals and told them not to fuss so." Bruce smiled thinking about it. "My father is already at the hospital so I'll ring him to see if he has any further news. I feel so useless being so far away." He pressed a couple of buttons on his phone and his father answered almost immediately.

Charlotte decided she'd be more useful getting on with the cocoa. A thought struck her and she opened her iPad and looked up flights to Scotland. There were flights the next day from Southampton to Edinburgh, which wasn't too far from Perth. Charlotte would suggest he goes and checks his mother himself. He may have worried about leaving the business, or her, so if she suggested it hopefully he'll realise it was a good idea. She hadn't heard much about Bruce's family in Scotland. Whenever he mentioned them Libby always seemed to cut him off mid-sentence. Bruce told Charlotte once that he thought Libby was almost ashamed by the fact she had married a Scotsman. Libby was such a snob. Friendlier people you would never meet than the Scots, her mother used to say. And she was always right when it came to judging people.

She was pouring the milk when Bruce walked into the kitchen.

"Just what the doctor ordered." He sat at the table and waited for Charlotte to sit with him and enjoy their cocoa. "My father is just leaving the infirmary, caught him just in time. Had a quick word with my mother; not a happy lady. She's been giving the doctors what for, 'for straining the NHS and keeping her there over night when she had a bed of her own waiting for her.' They'll be glad to say goodbye to her in the morning, I can tell you." Bruce had impersonated his mother to a T.

"I've had a thought." She told herself to tread carefully. "Why don't you hop on a flight tomorrow and surprise your mother? There's a flight to Edinburgh at lunchtime so you could be with them by teatime. I can handle work with George and if I have a query I can always phone you. I hear they have electricity in Scotland now." Bruce laughed. He had thought about it himself but didn't want to leave Charlotte alone with James' behaviour being so erratic.

"Brilliant idea. Let's book our seats now." He turned the iPad towards him and started typing.

"You need to go alone and check on your mother. They won't want me there." She rather liked the idea of going away with him though.

"They'll love it if I bring you. Anyway, I was going to book a couple of rooms in the Craigie Lodge, near Forfar where my parents live. You'll get a real feel of Scotland there. My cousin Archie owns it with his wife Helen." Bruce looked Charlotte in the eyes with a pleading expression. Charlotte laughed at his puppy dog eyes. She couldn't say no, she didn't want to say no.

"Yes, ok, if you think it would be appropriate, I'll come." Bruce smiled.

"Even if it is inappropriate you can come." Banter seemed to come naturally when they were alone.

They left for the airport in the morning after both of them had explained exactly where they were going and what needed to be done while they were away to George. She was delighted Bruce was taking Charlotte away for a few days.

She promised to phone if there was a problem, and to keep an eye on the house, and to keep an eye on Alan.

"For goodness sake Charlie, it's a couple of days not weeks. Just enjoy yourself and relax. Recharge your batteries, so to speak. And send my love to Bruce's family. Hopefully we can all meet them one day." Charlotte knew that was a sentence with many innuendos and that was exactly what George meant her to think. If she had been on a video call and not just audio, she'd swear her sister had winked at her.

The journey was amazingly easy. Flight arrived on time; car hire waiting for them and they arrived at the Craigie Lodge just in time for tea and scones. Archie fussed around them, pleased to see the cousin he'd grown up with.

After tea, Helen showed Charlotte up to her room. It was like going back in time. The throws on the bed were tartan and the bed looked so comfortable. There was a small armchair next to an open fire. It wasn't lit as the room was warmed by central heating, twenty-first century creeping in unobtrusively. The view from the window was like looking into a picture. Fir trees framed the border and fields with crops and sheep were focussed in the middle with a stream as a boundary from their garden. Charlotte looked back into the room and felt at home.

"What a beautiful room Helen. Thank you so much."

Helen looked at Charlotte. Her first thought was to make sure she fed her well before she left.

"Nae lass, I think we should be thanking you." Charlotte looked puzzled, until Helen carried on. "I've not seen Bruce so happy and with such a spring in his step since that woman dragged him down the aisle." She says it as it is, thought Charlotte, inwardly chuckling. "Our poor Aunty Bella, Bruce's mother, had hardly seen him in all the time they were married. Every time he managed to sneak up here for a few days he'd get a phone call to come home immediately because something bad had happened. One time it was the dishwasher had stopped working, I'm sure you ken what I mean." Charlotte really liked Helen. They were both laughing when Bruce walked in.

"I hope you're not regaling Charlotte with our childhood misdemeanours." Bruce turned to Charlotte. "In case you were wondering we were all in the same class from kindergarten through to senior school." Helen pointed out that in their village there was only one school.

"Which is why there is an abundance of nepotism in Angus." Bruce and Helen were laughing at their private joke. Charlotte sort of got it so smiled. "Anyway, I'm off to see my mother if you would like to come Charlotte?" Helen could see that Charlotte felt a little uncomfortable.

"She is looking forward to meeting you. We had a little chat this morning when I phoned to see how she was. She's fine by the way. You go off with Bruce, hen. We'll have a banquet ready for you when you get back." Helen was still worried about Charlotte's frame, certainly not robust enough to survive a highland winter.

"If you're sure. Then I'd love to come." Bruce took her by the arm and led her out to the car.

They drove past beautiful scenery and a field of the most magnificent herd of black cattle. Bruce caught a glimpse of Charlotte's face in absolute awe of the spectacle. He was so proud of his Scotland.

"Do you know what they are, besides the obvious?" Charlotte was tempted to say cows, but shook her head. "They are your actual Aberdeen Angus cattle seen in all their splendour in their native home. Born and bred here, just like me!"

"And magnificent specimens they are too." She was waiting for his response, and wasn't disappointed.

"Just like me!" Bruce in his own environment was even more attractive and lovable than she could have imagined. "If you look over the other side they are Aberdeen Angus too, but they are my favourite." Charlotte turned to see a field of red longhaired cattle.

"They all could do with a brushing." She was joking. They were just as magnificent. It made her think about becoming a vegetarian. Before she could think about the consequences of that thought her stomach turned over. They had pulled up outside a cottage. "There's my father. As usual, keeping out of the way." He was smiling. His father was on his knees weeding. As Charlotte got out of the car she could see it was a full-time job. The land stretched back acres and acres. Bruce had described his parents place as a smallholding. In England, it would be described as a farm!

"Hello, Dad. This is Charlotte." Charlotte went to shake hands with a slightly older version of Bruce, but he grabbed her into a bear hug. Like father, like son, she thought, feeling very relaxed and comfortable in this stranger's arms.

"How lovely to meet you, lassie. Bruce has been talking about nothing else and I can see why." Charlotte blushed as he let go of her and stood back to take a look at her. "Ay Bruce, she is bonny." Bruce winked at Charlotte. She grinned.

"Stop your blithering Johnny Gordon and get the lass in here before all the neighbours know our business." Bella was at the front door of the cottage with a big grin on her face.

"As you can see, the nearest neighbours are in the next town." Bruce tried to make Charlotte feel less nervous at meeting his mother, whose bark was worse than her bite. Bruce went over to his mother and lifted her off the ground. It was obvious that he had been worried and was pleased to see her looking well. "Och, be away with ye daft laddie." She planted a big kiss on his cheek before being put back down onto terra firma. "And this will be Charlotte?" Charlotte nodded.

"Hello Mrs Gordon, lovely to meet you." She put out her hand and somehow knew her head was going to end up in this lovely woman's cleavage.

"Mrs Gordon was my mither-in-law, I'm Bella. Now Charlotte let's get you both in and put the kettle on." Bella kept Charlotte in an embrace through to a quaint sitting room followed by Johnny with his arm around his son. Charlotte's first thought was that Bruce had had the same adoring family up bringing as she'd had. On one hand, it made her very happy but on the other it made her angry that Bruce had been put through so much pain from Libby.

No, she thought, she must get Libby and all English things out of her head and enjoy the moments in Scotland.

Bruce noticed his mother limping and while she went on into the kitchen with Charlotte he asked his father exactly what had happened.

"Ye know your mither and her sister." He tutted whilst shaking his head. "Too busy blethering to notice anything on the road. Well, a tractor pulled out of one of Jock Cameron's fields and because the roads were wet she slid straight into it. Luckily she had braked because I know what vehicle would have won in that altercation."

"So how did she get injured?"

"That's another story. She got out of the car and went to tell the driver off and slipped up on the slurry the tractor had brought out from the field. Twisted her ankle a treat. Funnily enough Flora got a neck strain and a nosebleed from the airbag, but your mother's didn't deploy. I can see her writing to the manufacturers for compensation. Not sure how that'll turn out for a strained ankle." He laughed to cover his concern that the accident could have been much worse and he'd be looking into the airbag situation himself.

"Come on you laddies, clear the table and sit yourselves doon." Bella had made the tea and Charlotte was carrying it on a tray for her so she could keep the weight of her ankle. The girls had been chatting in the kitchen and Bella had explained about her ankle. She also told her she had a lovely bruise on her bottom and her ego, but she wasn't going to tell the boys that! "So Bruce, you'll be taking Charlotte up to Arbroath tomorrow to see Hen and Ron?" Bruce knew he wouldn't get away with visiting Scotland without popping in to all the relatives. He wanted to anyway. He'd told

Charlotte about how his flat in Poole reminded him of his aunt and uncle's home in Arbroath so he wanted her to see for herself.

"It's on the agenda, Mither. Did ye and Faither want to come?" Charlotte had goosepimples. She loved the Scottish intonation.

"Och, ye two go. Johnny has to clean out the pullet house ready for the new batch." Johnny was nodding with a look of acceptance on his face. "And I will be busy writing a letter to the procurator fiscal about my air bag and the state of the lanes. If they kept the roads cleaner there'd be less accidents." Bruce looked at Charlotte and grinned. He was so glad Charlotte had gone with him to his home. He could never share it with his ex-wife. She was too rude and snobbish to enjoy the wonderful things in life that actually didn't cost a penny, like family, nature, friends and love. All of which were in Scotland in abundance for Bruce. It used to cost a fortune keeping Libby amused. He could see in Charlotte's eyes that she was very happy, just by being there with him and his family.

Bruce looked at his watch. Helen would have their dinner on the table soon. He had to say goodbye to his parents. Bella noticed him looking at the time and made it easy for him.

"Ye two had better be off or I'll have the wrath of Helen if your dinner ruins!" She was smiling. She'd enjoyed the visit more than they will know. She missed her Bruce, but her instinct told her she'd be seeing more of him in the future.

"Just let me carry these into the kitchen, and I'll be with you." Charlotte put the crockery onto the tray and made her way back to the kitchen. Bella followed her, leaving Bruce with his father chatting about the smallholding. Johnny needed his opinion on where to put the boundary for the sale of some of the land as it was getting too much for him and the next-door farmer had shown interest.

In the kitchen Bella was watching Charlotte wiping down the work surface and stacking the dishwasher that Bruce had finally persuaded them to have and he bought them only a year ago. Bella only used it on special occasions. Nothing got the cups clean like a good bit of elbow grease and scouring powder! That other woman didn't get off her backside except to leave, she thought.

"So Elizabeth was your best friend? I can't see ye two together. She was a snob. Never good enough for my Bruce." Charlotte had to agree with her. Libby was a snob. "And that James, what a galoot for letting a lovely lass like ye go." Bella noticed Charlotte's eyebrow rise. "Idiot." Charlotte understood. "Mind ye lass, one man's loss is another man's gain." She got up and hugged Charlotte. "A mither knows, and my lad is smitten." She winked at Charlotte, who beamed back at her. "Our secret, but I'm hoping we'll be seeing a lot more of you in the future lassie."

"I hope so too, Bella." They walked back out to find father and son in the garden pointing at fences. "I'm ready, Bruce." Charlotte kissed Bella and Johnny goodbye. Bruce picked his mother up and whispered in her ear. Charlotte couldn't hear what he said but his mother smiled and winked again at Charlotte. Very little conversation happened on the way back to Craigie Lodge, but both of them were smiling in amiable silence.

CHAPTER 13

Dinner was a feast. Archie and Helen joined them and the evening was delightful. Charlotte hadn't stopped laughing all through the anecdotes of their childhood. She was getting to know a different, mischievous side of Bruce. She realised that Bruce had been encouraged into the shenanigans (Helen's word) by his cousins with him being the youngest. They must have had so much fun.

"So, you're off to Arbroath to see my parents in the morning? You'll be introducing Charlotte to the Smokies then?" Bruce nodded.

"All I can say is that I hope they live up to all the hype they've had." Charlotte was intrigued that everyone from the area talked about Arbroath Smokies. Well tomorrow she would give them her opinion as a Sassenach.

They all said their goodnights and Bruce escorted Charlotte up to her room and opened her door for her.

"Thank you for coming up here with me. You have been a big hit with my family. Are you having a lovely time?" Bruce looked her in the eyes while he asked. His mother had always told him that the eyes couldn't lie. He got his answer straight away. Her eyes smiled. That was one thing he disliked about Libby, especially in company. She'd smile with her mouth but her eyes never smiled.

"I can't remember the last time I had such an incredible time. Your family are amazing and absolutely marvellously warm and kind and Scotland is glorious, no wonder you are so proud to be Scottish." Bruce was about to explode with love for this remarkable woman. He put an arm round her and held her close.

"I'm afraid I'm falling in love with you." Bruce whispered in her ear. Charlotte looked up and he noticed tears in her eyes.

"I know I'm in love with you. Who wouldn't be? You are the kindest, gentlest, most compassionate man I have ever met." With his left foot, he managed to shut the bedroom door. He gently lifted her chin up and stared into her eyes.

"I want to look after you and protect you for the rest of your life. I want to hold you every night until you go to sleep. I want to kiss you the noo." He saw her smile. No more words were needed. He bent forward and put his lips on hers. His tongue prized open her lips and the sensation made her knees go weak. He felt her relax and scooped her up onto the bed. She thought the experience she was feeling must be very near to what heaven was like. They took their time undressing and exploring each other's body and soul, starting slowly and building to a crescendo they both hoped no one could hear. Charlotte had never reached such heights and truly believed she was in a place called euphoria.

James got the distinct impression that he wasn't welcome at the Golf Club, and couldn't imagine why. He was immaculately dressed even to the point of gel in his hair to keep it smart. But he was definitely persona non grata. Ok, he'd let a few people down over the last month or so, but surely they could appreciate what he'd been through. Well sod them all, he thought. He didn't need any of the 'old boy network'. He left the club with no work and a very dented ego. He stopped at the off-licence on his way home and had to think of another plan. Getting clients back was not an option. The word had got out that he was unreliable. The death knell of the self-employed man. He needed money and the easiest way was from Charlie. He wanted a job; that was Charlie again. He wanted his life back as it was; again, Charlie was required for that too. He needed Charlie alone to work on her with the charm and charisma that first attracted her to him. If he couldn't get Bruce out of the way, he had to get Charlie away from Bruce. A plan was hatching in his warped brain. It could work. He realised he had nothing to lose. Yes, he thought, it's got to bloody well work. He opened his computer and typed 'Rohypnol'.

"Morning." Bruce was looking down on a very dishevelled Charlotte. Her hair was all over her face. He carefully pulled it from her eyes and smiled into them.

"Morning." She stretched and felt so relaxed that she didn't even pull the sheet over her nakedness. Bruce was drawing a heart with his finger on her stomach. She wriggled.

"Ooo, ticklish?" He loved that vulnerability in her. She was such a strong, independent woman, finding a little chink in her armour made him feel protective towards her. He kissed her and wanted to go further but was aware that they had overslept. "Breakfast will be on the table and my cousin will be up to see what's keeping us. Do you suppose I can ask for a rebate on the room we haven't used?" Charlotte laughed. "Tak' caur ay th' pennies an' th' poonds will tak' caur ay themselves." Bruce kissed her again and then got up and put a towel round his waist. He picked up his clothes and blew her a kiss at the door. "Give you twenty minutes to look even more radiant than you do at this moment, if that's possible." He left leaving Charlotte alone. The wonderful thing about what had happened in the last twelve hours was that she felt no guilt just contentment. She wanted to savour the moment and the feelings but knew she had to get into the shower. Begrudgingly she got herself up and started her day by texting her sister with the most rapturous message she'd sent in a long while.

Arbroath Smokies did not let her down. They were delicious. With Aunty Henny and Uncle Ronny sitting with them in a quaint sixteenth-century pub and guesthouse on the harbourfront, they were enjoying the lunchtime special. In the quiet moments Charlotte could hear the tinkle of the rigging on the masts of the boats in the harbour and totally understood Bruce's comparison with his home in Poole. Aunty Henny was the image of her sister Bella. They could be twins. Although Charlotte didn't say as much, Hennrietta was actually two years younger than her sister Isobella.

Aunty Henny regaled them with stories of Bruce when he stayed with them during the holidays. He, Archie and Roderick got up to so much mischief. She told her each of the incidences with a big smile on her face. The love for her nephew was evident.

With the promise of many more visits Bruce and Charlotte dropped them both off back to their cottage, the other side of the harbour and made their way back to the airport. They had plenty of time, but from past experience Bruce wanted to get over the Forth Road Bridge before he relaxed, especially with a plane to catch.

Charlotte felt she hadn't had time to draw breath or talk about the night before. She hoped he wasn't regretting it, but if body language was to be believed, he wasn't. He had been so thoughtful and caring all day. He was anxious to get to the airport on time so she didn't want to distract him.

"That was a big sigh." Bruce was watching her from the corner of his eye. "Have you had a lovely day?"

"I've had a lovely few days. I don't want to go home." She sighed again. "I wish we could live in Scotland." She looked up at his face. He was smiling.

"Scotland can do that to people. We'll be back soon, if you'd like that?" She nodded. "I need to help my father sort out this land business. I don't want him being ripped-off. The smallholding is far too big for him now. They could survive on half the land easily. It's just a question of which half." Charlotte had a radical idea.

"Bruce, what if we bought the other half and built a holiday cottage in the grounds? Would we be allowed to do that? Then we could pop up more frequently and you could help your dad." She realised she was being very presumptuous but Bruce usually liked her proposals.

"Brilliant idea, Charlotte." He was thrilled at the prospect of more visits with her to Scotland. "You do come up with some clever ideas. We'll look into it as soon as we get back. Ye canny lassie! I'm making the most of it before we cross the border." They had arrived at the car drop-off point at the airport in plenty of time. A little womble through Duty Free was in order, she thought. She decided to get Bruce a nice bottle of aftershave to thank him for bringing her to bonny Scotland.

George and Tom were at the house waiting for them. George had looked up the flight time and took into account the traffic. They had been there for enough time to get out the glasses and open a bottle of champagne.

"Are you sure this isn't a little overkill, Georgie?" Tom was so not a romantic, she thought.

"Absolutely not. Do you know how long I've waited for these two to get together? They were made for each other. They just needed to work it out themselves." Tom had to agree. It was the best outcome from the whole sordid mess that he called Libbygate.

"Hellooo." Charlotte had seen Tom's car outside. "Anybody home?" She walked into the lounge and found her sister and brother-in-law standing with smug faces. Her eyes moved to the coffee table with a tray and flutes filled with what had to be champagne. For one moment she thought perhaps George had some good news. But as soon as Bruce came in to join them George offered Charlotte a glass and Tom passed one over to Bruce.

"To my sister and our bestest friend in the world Bruce. Here's to love!" They chinked their glasses. "About bloody time too!" They all laughed. Bruce took hold of Charlotte and whispered in her ear.

"I take it it's legitimate then? No need to be furtive at work. They all know I'm bonking the boss?" Charlotte couldn't help herself. She sprayed her champagne over Bruce. She had tried not to laugh, but he had the most humorous turn of phrase. "By the way," he was still whispering, "I love you."

She turned round and kissed him passionately on the lips.

"Oh, get a room you two." Tom faked embarrassment. He was just as pleased as George that his friend and sister-in-law were now an item. "Come on George. Let's leave the lovebirds alone. Night you two. Don't do anything I wouldn't do, which obviously leaves you a lot of scope!" Bruce shook Tom's hand while the sisters cuddled. They left the lovebirds in peace.

Bruce refilled Charlotte's glass and handed it to her. "To us. New beginnings." Charlotte chinked his glass and nodded.

"Out with the old, in with the new." They chinked again. Bruce took her glass out of her hand and pulled her into an embrace that she didn't want to leave. For the first time in a very long while she felt secure, happy and unconditionally loved.

After perusing the internet, James found getting hold of any sort of prescription-only drug was nearly impossible from legal channels. He was quite concerned as to the contraindications too, which included respiratory depression and in rare cases cardiac failure including cardiac arrest. He didn't want to kill Charlie. No, he had to think of another way to get her on her own to convince her to let him back into her life.

He was interrupted from his thoughts by his mobile ringing. He looked to see who it was. The name L. Darling flashed on the screen. He made a note to delete that contact as soon as he'd answered it.

"What do you want, Libby dear?" The sarcasm in his voice was obvious. Libby was shocked at how bitter it sounded. She knew straight away she wasn't going to get an apology from him.

"Hello James. Just to let you know I got home safely the other night, in case you were worried." It was her turn for sarcasm. *"I also wanted to tell you that this number will be unavailable after this call as I have changed it. I do not want to hear from you again. I have been encouraged by Bruce and Charlotte to go to the police to press charges after your outrageous treatment of me the other evening, resulting in a very nasty cut on my leg."* She stopped for a moment to take a deep breath. He was quiet, she wondered if he was still there. *"But I don't think it will be necessary to give them a statement, will it? After all I will not be bothered by you again, will I?"* She couldn't believe how strong she sounded. She only hoped James was convinced she was adamant. If he could see her shaking and barely holding her phone steady he would realise she was bluffing. She would have been far too embarrassed to go to the police.

"Fair enough. Goodbye Libby." And he hung up.

"Bastard." She shouted, but knew he hadn't heard. What

on earth had possessed her to swap Bruce for that disgusting, despicable, disreputable, dirt bag she'll never know. She prided herself on her alliteration skills. They gave emphasis when it was needed. She turned off her phone and switched the SIM card with the new one, ending her relationship with James forever.

That was a strange little phone call. He couldn't understand what it was about. He had already dumped Libby, figuratively and literally. The fact Charlotte and Bruce had put their oar in he couldn't fathom. Why would they encourage Libby to go to the police? He had to get her out of the car she was annoying him. It's not like he dumped her in the middle of a desert, it was on a bus route after all. They were all making him out to be the bad guy. Now he had every right to play dirty. The gloves were off. He went back to the computer and looked for a way of getting his hands on some Rohypnol. According to the chat room he found the best place was outside a well-known nightclub in the centre of town. He'd give that a go. He checked through his small wardrobe to find a suitable outfit. Suit or casual chinos were out. He'd look like an undercover cop and stick out like a sore thumb. He found an old pair of jeans he used for washing the car and gardening when he lived with Libby. He had a sweatshirt and what technically could be called a hoodie, but was actually a golf kagool. Perfect, he looked the part of a clubber, although slightly older than the usual clientele. He'd give it a go once it was dark. At least then it would be more difficult for the supplier to see his face. Adrenalin was pumping through his body at a rate of knots. He'd sorted the method of capture. He now had to work out a plan of how and where to take her. Where was easy. He went into the Airbnb website and put Dorset in the search, then refined it to a secluded two-bedroom cottage with garage. He had to hide the car once there. There were three hits. Two of them needed the owner to accept the booking. The last one could be booked immediately. He booked it for three nights. If he hadn't changed her mind by then, he knew he'd have to think of something more drastic. He entered his credit card details and the booking was confirmed. He then got an email from the owner, Peter, explaining that the cottage was hidden from the road so attached was a map. An extra bonus, thought James. The email also told him that there was a key safe in the outside meter cupboard by the side of the kitchen door. He also gave him the code for the safe. Peter wished him a pleasant stay and told him to contact him if there was anything he could help with. James had to laugh. He wondered if Peter could help with the seducing of his ex-wife. Perhaps not, he'd do that himself.

Right, that's the where, what about the how? He had to think what would bring Charlie out without causing her to be suspicious. James suddenly had a light bulb moment. Libby, he thought. Libby mentioned something about going to the police to give a statement about his hurting her leg? He hadn't a clue what she was talking about, but what if she asked for Charlie's help to make the statement. She could get Charlie to meet her somewhere public like a restaurant and it'll be James there instead of Libby. He had a thought, he went into Yahoo and typed Libby's name, then the password she used on everything. She was so blonde, he thought. But for once it had worked on his side. He was into her email account. He had to calm down and formulate the most convincing plea to Charlie for help.

Dear Charlie, I'm sorry to trouble you again, but I've been thinking about the police statement and I need some help with it. Can we meet for lunch tomorrow while it is still fresh in my mind? I can book a table at La Pizzeria Roma, the one on the promenade for 12.30 if that's ok?

James was very pleased with it so far. He needed to end it like Libby would.

Lots of love, Libby. X

No, that didn't look right. Then he remembered the 'as always'.

Lots of love, as always, Libby. X

That was it. Perfect he thought, and pressed the send button. He immediately deleted it from Libby's account so she would have no idea what he'd done in her name. He'd leave the account open so he could get the answer then delete it.

He decided to go early the next morning to the cottage and check to see if he was going to have to do any DIY to keep her there. He needed to get supplies if they were going to be there long. She may agree to come back to him sooner than he thought; he doubted it would be that easy though. But then he liked a challenge.

He had a few hours before he could search for the drugs, so he kept an eye on Libby's email page and fine-tuned the rest of his scheme.

Charlotte didn't reply to the email until eight o'clock that evening. James was almost beside himself. He couldn't think of any other way to get Charlie away from her new minder, Bruce. Luckily, he was about to go out when he saw the message arrive in Libby's inbox.

Libby. I will help you on this occasion, but be aware that my patience is wearing thin. I have troubles of my own. I do not need yours too, as you have brought them on yourself.

That aside, I will be at the restaurant at the allotted time.

Yours Charlotte

James was surprised at how much Charlotte still loathed Libby. Extraordinary how women took everything to heart, he felt. He deleted the message and signed out of Libby's account. He telephoned the restaurant and booked a table for two in Libby's name, in a quietest spot, for 12.30 the next day. He collected his wallet with, he hoped, enough money to cover the street as opposed to online drug price and left on his mission.

CHAPTER 14

Charlotte was annoyed. When would Libby stop pestering her and Bruce? If Libby was in danger or injured of course she and Bruce would both go to her aid, but Libby was an intelligent woman, perhaps lapsed over the last few months, but she was quite capable of filling in a form. She was still annoyed when Bruce walked in from a late meeting with the accountant. He went up behind Charlotte and kissed her on her neck. Usually Charlotte moaned and surrendered into his caress. Not this time, Bruce noticed.

"What's happened? What's got you all upset?" She turned to face him and kissed him.

"Sorry, but it's your ex. She wants me to meet her for lunch at Pizzeria Roma, to help her with the statement to the police. It worries me that she can't do it herself. She's just attention seeking. I thought she'd grow out of that when we left kindergarten." She smiled. She had got it out of her system. She couldn't stay angry for long with Bruce standing looking so concerned. "I'll feel better when you've poured me a drink and told me how you got on at the accountants."

Bruce poured the drinks and took them into the lounge.

"He's very pleased with us. All the books were in order and we've done most of his job for him." Charlotte smiled. "And I got an A* too!" Bruce grinned.

"That's how to run a good business. Keep your hand on the pulse. Once they have been audited they can go back into the filing cabinet." Work was her therapy, that and the glass of wine! She was happy again. "I'll get this lunch over with Libby and make sure she realises that she's going to have to stand on her own two feet soon." Bruce agreed. It was getting tiresome.

"Do you want me to come too?" Charlotte shook her head.

"That's probably what she's hoping for. No, I'll deal with her. You go and relax on the golf course, or take a boat out for a little sail around the harbour. Don't worry about me; I'll be fine. I'll wave to you from the restaurant." He leant over her and tickled her into submission. "I'm only joking. I know you have a busy day tomorrow. Let's have an early night." Bruce stood up.

"Early night, early night?" he said winking at her. She laughed.

"Let me get dinner organised and we'll see how much time is left." He grabbed her and kissed her on the cheek. "The longer we are down here, the less time we'll have up there." He let go of her and gently guided her into the kitchen.

Charlotte was up bright and early the next morning. She had to go to Georgina's to meet a publisher friend who was coming down from London. It was a mutually beneficial meeting so she didn't mind leaving early for lunch with Libby. Georgina would cope brilliantly without her sister breathing down her neck. In fact, if the truth be known, Charlotte had to admit that George knew more about the publishing side of things than she did. Her forte was the business side, but she liked to keep an eye on all aspects of the company.

James arrived at the restaurant with a little jewellery box in his pocket. A brilliant touch, he thought. He'd parked his car cleverly behind the restaurant that was for staff only. There was no one around to notice. It was also free. Charlotte would park in the carpark opposite. Luckily the season was well and truly over so it was almost deserted.

There were a few people already sitting down eating. They were a mixture of older people and university students. The older people were talking to each other, the students were all on gadgets, probably just ordering coffees and taking advantage of the free wi-fi. James went to the bar and waited for the waiter.

"Hello sir, can I get you something?" James noted the tag on the lad's shirt 'Marco'.

"Thank you, Marco, I'd like a bottle of white wine, opened and set on the table in the name of Libby Gordon." He wanted Charlie to ask for the table when she arrived so it had to be in Libby's name. "And I'll have a small beer too." The waited gave him the beer and took the wine over to the table behind a pillar. Not exactly secluded, but the restaurant was round and surrounded by windows. No quiet corner so the pillar would have to do. When Marco returned James got out the little box.

"Now this is a secret between you and me. So, I need you to stay away from the table for a while. We'll order when she's hopefully said yes." Marco was excited. He was Italian and very romantic.

"If we do not have many customers I will make sure you are alone. Can I get you some champagne ready sir?" James was hoping after a glass of wine they'd be gone.

"No thank you. We will have to celebrate later, we are both driving." James asked for the bill so far.

"I'll pay for the wine and beer now, I want to use cash. I'm going to put the food on my expense account." He wanted to pay for the drinks so they could leave when the plan was working. Marco nodded, totally understanding the situation.

James went over to the table and filled the glass for Charlie. He carefully managed to add the drug he had crushed back at the flat, without being seen. He poured himself half a glass to make it look like Libby had already started.

He went back over to the waiter who was busy making espressos and got his attention.

"Now my girlfriend will be arriving and asking for the table booked in the name of Libby Gordon. Can you take her over and tell her Mrs Gordon won't be long, she'd just popped to the car to put a ticket on it in the carpark." Marco was eager to help make it the most amazing surprise. He was nodding frantically. James had to go before Charlie arrived. He handed Marco a fiver and left.

Charlotte arrived bang on 12.30 and put the coins in the meter for the carpark. She placed the ticket on her dashboard and locked the door. Walking over to the restaurant she couldn't help facing the sea and taking a few deep breaths. It really was invigorating, and she'd need all the energy she could get to deal with Libby. As she walked through the door a waiter almost ran over to her. Such good service she thought.

"Hello, have you a table booked in the name of Libby Gordon?" Marco was nodding.

"*Si, si, bella.* This way." He led her to the table and sat her at the full glass of wine, with her back to the entrance. "Mrs Gordon will not be long, she had to put change in the carpark. Please enjoy the wine while you wait for her." Marco was grinning from ear to ear. Luckily Charlotte assumed it was because he was Italian. "*Ciao, bella Signora.*" He was being signalled by a customer and left her alone.

She noticed that Libby had started on the wine already, so took a sip of her own. The menus were tablemats, very ingenious. She looked to see what salads they had. She briefly wondered why she hadn't seen Libby in the carpark, then decided she may have been in one of the beach kiosks asking for change.

After a couple of sips of wine, which in her opinion wasn't tasting any better being left to breathe, she wondered whether Libby had got lost. She was about to turn round to look for her when a hand went onto her shoulder. Then a voice sent warning shots through her psyche.

"Hello Charlie, so glad you could make it." She was about

to get up when James continued. "Please stay there while I explain why I'm here. Feel free to leave after you have heard me out." Charlotte was very angry. She had been tricked. Surely Libby hadn't helped to arrange the deception. "Before you start hating Libby more than you already do, she knows nothing about today. I used her email account to arrange it all. Perhaps if you see her you can tell her she ought to change her password." He grinned. Charlotte didn't want to know the password, but it was obvious James wanted to tell her. "LDarling007. Ironic that it came in useful, don't you think?" James Bond he was not. Chivalrous, suave and debonair are not qualities that came to mind when thinking of James Whitfield. Charlotte was getting bored with James's company.

"If you want me to hear what you went to all this trouble to arrange, get on with it." She stifled a yawn and shook her head. Perhaps she'd have to have an early night, without playtime, she thought. Why was she so tired? She took another sip of wine hoping it would restore her energy.

James knew exactly what was happening. He thought it would take longer, but she hadn't eaten and alcohol sped up the process according to the Internet.

"I wanted to talk to you about a reconciliation." And take as long as he could.

Charlotte didn't want to hear any more. She went to pick up her phone, but before she reached it James had already swiped it off the table. "You can have it back once you've heard me out. I promise." He sounded like a schoolboy, only it wasn't a football they were talking about, it was her lifeline. She needed to get it back to try and tape him, or at least take a photo to prove he was there. She sat back as if to give him permission to carry on. She wasn't feeling right so wanted to get it over with as soon as she could.

"Go on then." She heard herself slurring. She'd only had a glass of wine, but felt rather drunk. James was staring at her. She tried to focus to see his expression. She was sure he was smiling.

"I want to apologise again. You don't seem to understand how sorry I am for my behaviour. Apparently the internet said it could be the male menopause, like a mid-life crisis."

"Don't be so stupid James. You are far too young to have a mid-life crisis. Just admit to yourself that you are just a contemptible arse and perhaps you will be half way to passing as a human being again." She yawned again, James carried on.

"You're right, of course. I realise that now. I'm going to get help and perhaps we could go to some therapy classes together like Relate? It could help us get back to where we were." Charlotte shook her head and wished she hadn't. That wine was strong, she thought.

"You live in cloud cuckoo land James. Now I really would like my phone back." She wanted to call Bruce. She wasn't feeling right at all and needed to get away from James.

"So you don't think we can be together again, ever? But surely for old times' sake we could be friends?" James was trying to look appealing, almost cute, but it wasn't working. What was working was his delaying tactic. Charlotte was struggling to stay awake.

"No James, not at the moment. Perhaps in the future, who knows, but for now please give me my phone back and pay the bill. I obviously do not want anything to eat." She couldn't have eaten even if she had wanted too. Her mouth was feeling dry. Her head was all over the place. She wanted to call Bruce. James handed her the phone just out of reach. Charlotte made an attempt to grab it but couldn't focus on it.

"Are you ok Charlie? Do you need some fresh air?" He needed to time it so she wasn't completely useless, but also wasn't able to protest. Charlotte tried to turn to see if she could see the waiter. She needed to get help. James got up and pulled her round to face him. "Now listen. I'm going to take you outside for some fresh air. Then I'll help you to your car." He made sure she saw him put her phone in her handbag. He was lulling her into a false sense of security so she didn't make a scene until they were out of sight of the restaurant. Charlotte couldn't stand. Her legs felt like jelly. The restaurant seemed like it was one of those revolving ones. James helped her up and signalled to the waiter that he was just taking her outside for some fresh air. Marco came over to help.

"She's feeling faint. She couldn't believe it. Completely shocked, bless her. She'll be fine once she's been outside." James was very convincing. He kept Charlotte's head down so she couldn't make eye contact with Marco. The expression of abject horror on her face couldn't have been disguised.

Charlotte felt the air changing and knew she was outside. She couldn't get her mind to function properly. She wasn't focussing or processing her movements. She just wanted to go to sleep. James managed to prop her up against the car while he got his keys out. She was slithering down but he managed to straighten her and turn her, aiming her bottom onto the seat, whilst holding her head so as not to crack it on the doorframe. That would just make her compos mentis, which he didn't want to do.

By the time James had got Charlotte settled and he'd driven out of the staff carpark, Charlotte was asleep. His heart was pumping so fast he thought he'd have a heart attack. He didn't feel guilty leaving the restaurant. He'd given Marco a tip earlier and they had a half bottle of wine for their trouble. He kept checking Charlotte was still breathing. He was worried about the contraindications of the drug but thus far all seemed okay. The amount he had given her should keep her quiet for at least a couple of hours. Enough time to get her settled in the cottage and shut away from outside influence. Once it was just the two of them there together, James knew he had a better chance of getting the passion back into their relationship.

He drove out of the town and into the countryside. It took thirty minutes to get to the cottage, mainly because he was stuck behind a milk tanker most of the way. The expletives he was muttering would have shocked all of Mrs Brown's Boys!

When he finally got to the cottage he opened the door and went back for Charlotte. He struggled to get her out of the car without disturbing her. Unfortunately, she had a few bumps on the way up the stairs, especially as there were two sets. On the first floor were the main bedrooms and the next floor, which was a converted attic, had been made into a spare bedroom. Luckily there were no windows apart from a Velux in the attic. There was also a small en suite shower room in the corner that had a Velux window. From an imprisoning point of view the room was perfect. No windows to escape from, and only one door to the landing. James had put a bolt on the outside that morning. He would probably lose his deposit for defacing the doorframe with screw holes and a bolthole, but he didn't care.

Laying her carefully on the bed, he decided it would be better to keep her fully clothed. He didn't want her to think he'd taken advantage of her and get her agitated before he had started negotiations to resume their marriage.

He needed her to be disorientated which the darkness would do if she stayed asleep for a few more hours, so he took her watch off and put it in his pocket. Her phone was still in her bag, he decided to leave all that in the car. His theory was that the more confused she became, the more likely she was to feel close to the only person there. He was banking on the Stockholm syndrome taking effect. James fantasised during the planning stage that the abductee would fall for the abductor. He left her with a change of clothing still in the shop bags in the drawers and bolted her door from the outside. He had to put the car into the garage before the alarm was raised and a vigilant local bobby spotted it.

He took a look outside and was very pleased with his choice. The nearest neighbour was out of shouting distance. Behind the house was the main London – Weymouth line. The noise of frequent trains would cover any shouts and screams. He gave himself a nonliteral pat on the back. He couldn't believe it had worked. There were so many complications that could have happened but they didn't. Probably because no one would expect a sane man to kidnap his ex-wife in broad daylight in front of a restaurant half full of people. But he had. The next part wasn't going to be so easy. But he had faith in his ability to charm.

CHAPTER 15

Bruce got home quite early. He felt like a teenager wanting to be with his girlfriend as often as he could. Disappointment suddenly took the smile off his face. Charlotte's car was not there. Maybe she was at George's, he'd check inside to see if she had left a note. After half an hour, having found no clue as to her whereabouts, he phoned her. There was no answer and it went to voicemail.

"Hello gorgeous. Just wondered where you were and if lunch had gone okay. See you soon. Ps. I love you."

Now he was worried. He phoned George next. She hadn't seen or heard from her since she left for a lunch meeting. Bruce didn't want to worry her unduly so told her she'd probably stopped off at the supermarket as they were running low of dishwasher tablets. Did he really say dishwasher tablets? Well, it had worked. George told him she'd tell Charlotte he was looking for her if she called.

He opened Charlotte's iPad. Luckily there was no security password, as she knew Bruce had to use it for the business too. He scanned through her emails. From lunchtime, no emails had been opened. That was suspicious in itself. Charlotte checked her mail regularly. He went over the conversation with Libby in case the venue and time had changed for their meeting. He shook his head. The last email was from Charlotte:

"Libby. I will help you on this occasion, but be aware that my patience is wearing thin. I have troubles of my own. I do not need yours too, as you have brought them on yourself.

That aside, I will be at the restaurant at the allotted time.

Yours Charlotte"

Bruce telephoned Libby's mobile to see if they were still together. He got an unobtainable tone. He started to panic. He phoned the landline. No answer.

He left it for as long as he could, which was another ten minutes and decided to go out and search for her in case she had broken down. He took her iPad with him to keep an eye on her Internet activity. If she answered any of her mail he'll know she was okay. First stop would be Pizzeria Roma and work his way back from there. She couldn't possibly still be there but it was a good place to start.

As he pulled up in the carpark he caught sight of Charlotte's car. She was still there. Perhaps the girls had made up. Bruce thought that unlikely. As he parked next to her car he noticed a parking ticket on the windscreen wiper still in its waterproof cover. Charlotte would normally have popped out and put more money in the machine. That's what she usually did. He checked the time on the ticket in case the warden was being pedantic. She may have topped it up but missed a few minutes. He read the time on the original ticket on the windscreen 12.30 hrs. She'd paid for an hour. Something was wrong. There was no way she'd have left it that long. Normally she would have phoned the number and paid by card, but for one hour she probably thought it was not worth it. He walked into the restaurant.

He went over to the waitress behind the bar.

"Excuse me. Did you see a couple of ladies having lunch on a table booked in the name of Gordon at 12.30 today?" The waitress looked clueless.

"I wasn't here at lunchtime. I've just come on duty." Bruce noticed three other waiters attending to customers.

"Anyone here on duty at lunchtime?" The waitress looked around and spotted Marco. She pointed to him.

"Marco has been on duty all day." She shouted over to Marco. "Marco, can you come and talk to this gentleman please?" Marco excused himself from a conversation he was having with a customer and went over to the bar. He put an enormous black pepper mill down on the counter.

"*Si signore.* Can I help you?" Bruce repeated the question he had asked the waitress. "No *signore.* I saw one lady and one gentleman. It was supposed to be a lady but the *signore* had surprised her. He was going to ask her to marry him, I thought so romantic, but no. They seemed to be having an argument and she did not look happy. She then was very sleepy, weak? How do you say?" The waitress helped him.

"Faint?"

"*Si*, fainty. He helped her outside. I did not see them again." He shook his head and looked worried. He should have paid more attention, but the restaurant was getting busy and he was serving on his own.

"When you say helped her, did she go willingly?" Bruce was beginning to have a panicky feeling about the scenario just explained to him.

"I don't think she was very, how do you say, *sveglio*... awake." Marco was worried he'd get the blame so tried to cover himself. "It wasn't anything she had eaten *signore*, she hadn't ordered food, just wine. She only had a glass. Most of the bottle was left." Bruce was holding it together, just. His first thought was that Charlotte had been drugged.

"Can you describe the man to me?" He knew it was James before he asked. Then Marco described him to a T. Bruce thanked him and ran out of the restaurant.

He drove to the police station. It had been over six hours since James had driven off with Charlotte. He tried ringing Charlotte again on his hands free. No answer. Libby's mobile still had no tone. He tried the landline.

"Hello Bruce, how are you?" At last, she was home.

"Have you seen or heard from either James or Charlotte today?" No time for niceties.

"I spoke to James yesterday. I told him that I was changing my mobile number so he couldn't pester me and I also told him that you and Charlotte had told me to report him to the police. I wanted to scare him into leaving me alone. I told him that if he kept away I wouldn't press charges. That was it really. Why?"

"So, you didn't send Charlotte an email asking her to lunch?" Bruce already knew the answer. It didn't take a genius to hack into an email account, especially if you knew your way around computers and you'd lived with the account holder.

"No I didn't. Bruce, are you going to tell me what's going on?" Bruce was tempted but just in case Libby was in cahoots with James he played it safe.

"James is playing silly buggers, that's all. Speak soon." He was gone, without even a goodbye. Libby was completely confused. But she looked down at her nails and they were lovely. All afternoon she had been at the spa. She deserved it after the week she had had.

Bruce pulled up outside the police station and parked in a 'visitors only' space that gave him twenty minutes. He walked into the reception area and up to the window.

"Can I help you sir?" There was a man sitting the other side, in civilian clothes.

"I want to report a missing person, or it may be a kidnapping." He was getting too anxious. He needed to talk to a police officer. "It's urgent."

"Can I have your name please, sir?" This was going to take ages.

"My name is Bruce Gordon. My girlfriend's name is Charlotte Whitfield and her ex-husband has taken her somewhere and we need to find her." He was getting louder and louder but couldn't help it.

"Right sir, try to calm down. Now how long has Mrs Whitfield been missing?" Bruce checked his watch.

"Over six hours." It didn't sound a lot, but it was not the time it was what he was doing to her that was the urgency.

"I'm sorry sir but she is an adult and unless she has been missing for twenty-four hours we don't usually get too concerned. I would suggest you go home and wait. You know what women are like. She's probably got chatting to a friend and lost all concept of time" He was making jokes, for God's sake.

"You don't understand. She is in danger. We are in the middle of getting a restraining order out against her ex-husband. He has taken her somewhere and God knows what he's doing to her." He was shouting without realising it.

"Can you wait there one moment, sir." The receptionist pointed to the row of chairs. Bruce realised he'd finally got through to him. A slight exaggeration about the restraining order may have done the trick, but he was desperate. He got out his phone and rung Jeremy; he'll be the best person to help. Jeremy answered straight away. He was on his way home. Bruce tried to summarise what had happened at Restaurant Roma and his concern for Charlotte's safety. Jeremy promised to turn his car around immediately and would be at the station in no longer than ten minutes.

A policeman opened the side door and motioned to Bruce.

"Follow me sir, if you please." Bruce did as he was told. He felt like a zombie. The whole episode was unreal and difficult to process. He had to stay focussed and strong, for Charlotte's sake. The officer led him to an interview room and offered him glass of water. "Now sir, can you explain your concerns for..." he looked down at his paperwork, "Mrs Whitfield."

He told the police officer what had been happening in Charlotte's life recently and said how worried he was for Charlotte's safety as James had been acting unbalanced for some time. He took out Charlotte's iPad and showed the officer Charlotte's emails and told him that Libby had not sent them. Bruce told him that James was a computer expert and could hack into any account but probably knew Libby's password anyway.

"It was a ruse to get Charlotte alone. James knew she would help Libby no matter how betrayed she felt." The officer was busy writing it all down. Bruce felt a little easier that someone was taking him seriously. But the whole process was taking too long. He needed them to get out there and start searching for her.

"So, you got home, found her missing, made some phone calls which were fruitless, then what did you do?" The officer looked up at Bruce. He could see Bruce was agitated but he needed to get the facts down before they could investigate further.

"I decided to go to the last place I knew she had been, then work my way back. That was the restaurant. There I found her car in the carpark but no sign of her. She hadn't been back to her car since she'd left it at 12.30. She had a parking ticket to prove it. I then went into the restaurant to check she wasn't there and talked to the waiter who had served her called Marco."

He then explained what the waiter had told him at the restaurant.

"I know she's been kidnapped. She must have been drugged. She would not have gone voluntarily with that man. We've got to find her." Bruce put his head in his hands. He was trying not to keep it together but he was feeling so frustrated.

There was a knock at the door and Jeremy had arrived followed by a detective. Jeremy went over and shook Bruce's hand and sat down with him. The detective had been talking to Jeremy and had got the gist of what had been happening.

He checked with the officer to see how much more information he had.

"Right sir. I am DS Mellowes, and I'm taking over your case. I need to know Mr Whitfield's address and his car registration. His mobile phone number would be useful too and Mrs Whitfield's." He went over to Bruce. "Trust us sir. I've got officers already on their way to pick up the CCTV tape from the restaurant and have it in motion to get the council one of the carpark. We will find them." He had his hand on Bruce's shoulder. "Now sir, it would be better for you to go home and wait there. Stay close to the phone in case either contact you."

"James isn't after a ransom. He just wants Charlotte back. And at the moment he has her." Bruce sounded totally defeated. Jeremy helped him up.

"They know what they are doing Bruce. Come on, let's go back to Charlotte's and wait there. We can do no more than get out of the way and let the police do what they are good at." Bruce nodded. Jeremy was right.

"Thank you." Bruce shook the detective's hand and then the officer's. Jeremy walked him to his car. "I better let Georgina and Tom know what's happening. Not sure if I should ring Alan. After the last scare with Charlotte I'm not sure how he'll take it." Jeremy agreed.

"I'll pop round to Alan's and explain exactly what has gone on. Then I'll bring him round to you, don't want him driving in the state of mind he'll be in." Bruce thanked him. As he drove home he telephoned George and told her Charlotte was missing and he feared James had abducted her. By the time he got back to Charlotte's, George and Tom were already at the house waiting to be put in the picture.

Shortly after Jeremy arrived with Alan. Tom poured everyone a brandy. It had been quite a shock and he thought it would help.

"So, has anyone any idea as to where he would take her?" Bruce couldn't stop his brain working. No one could help. Apart from his flat that was rented, James didn't have any property. He could have rented another but he didn't have the money. The only feasible explanation was that he'd got a short-term holiday let. Somewhere he could pay cash for.

"Like an Airbnb. No questions asked just money up front." George and Tom had stayed in an Airbnb for a couple of days in London. "The anonymity would be ideal for a kidnap." It didn't help though. There was no way of checking unless they had his account details, if indeed he had rented somewhere. They were all deep in their own thoughts when the doorbell rang. George ran to the door. A uniformed woman officer was standing there with a detective. They showed her their badges.

"Please come in, we're all in the lounge, this way." Bruce got up and shook the detective's hand.

"This is DS Mellowes everyone." DS Mellowes went round the room shaking their hands. He introduced PC Catling to them.

"Can I get you a cup of tea or coffee?" George wanted to keep busy. PC Catling took off her jacket.

"Leave it to me. You need to stay in here and listen to what DS Mellowes has to tell you." She left the room on a mission to find the kitchen.

"Now then, we are waiting for Mercedes to come back to us with the position of Mr Whitfield's car." They all looked surprised. "With the registration number, we were able to ascertain that his model has a GPS tracker system on it. Mercedes will only give out the information with the relevant legal documents. They don't give it to wives trying to catch their husbands out, as you can imagine, so we have to go down the data protection route. They now have the information they need. We should get the position of the vehicle back any time now." George went over and hugged Bruce. She thought he needed one. He was looking so anxious, understandably. "As soon as we have any further information we'll let PC Catling know and she can tell you. I'm leaving her here with you just in case Mr Whitfield tries to contact you." PC Catling came in with a tray of coffees, a sugar bowl and some digestive biscuits.

"Right Madonna, I'm going back to the station. Be back for you later."

"Okay, sarge." She smiled at him. He was quite attractive in a manly way, perhaps a bit too old for her though. She guessed he was over thirty.

DS Mellowes grabbed a digestive and left.

"Is that your name, Madonna?" Tom was fascinated. She looked a little young to be a Madonna but maybe her mother was a fan.

"I've only just passed out from training. This is my first station. They've all been very kind to me but I'm afraid I was immediately given the nickname Madonna." She found it rather amusing.

"Why Madonna?" George wondered if she could sing.

"Because I'm a newbie. 'Like a Virgin'?" she spelled it out. The penny dropped. For a few moments, they forgot their worries and laughed. George thought PC Catling was going to make a very good officer.

CHAPTER 16

~

Charlotte could hear a voice calling her name. It seemed to be in the distance. Perhaps it was her mother. She hated getting up for school. Not like her older sister. Georgina was up with the larks and dressed ready for school and normally reading one of their mother's old, smelly books, at the breakfast table. Charlotte loved her bed. She snuggled down further. An odd thought floated into her mind, had her mother changed the washing powder? It smelled different. She could hear her name again, only it couldn't be her mother, it was a man's voice. It must be her father. But that was odd; he was usually at work before Charlotte had to get up, unless he was on nights in the control tower, then he wasn't back before she'd left for school. Nothing was making sense. That voice, it was familiar. Almost instinctively she sat bolt upright. It was James's voice. She saw a silhouette of a person on the bottom of her bed in the glow of the open door. It was dark in the room.

"Hello darling, how are you feeling?" James was playing on the fact that Charlotte was disorientated. "You've had a funny turn, but you look better now." James handed her a glass of water.

Charlotte's mind was trying to put everything into a logical order. Where was she? Why was she with James? How did she get there? What was the last clear thing she remembered? That helped. The last thing she remembered was sitting in a restaurant waiting for Libby. Or was she? She didn't see Libby. No, because James was there. That's it, it was getting clearer, James had planned the meeting. What did she do there? She was trying to think, ignoring James's voice. She didn't want to talk. She had to think. Wine, she remembered, she drank a glass of wine. She hadn't eaten food, just drank wine. That was the last thing she remembered.

She put the glass of water down as it suddenly dawned on her that the wine could have been drugged. She needed to clear her head if she was going to get out of the situation, whatever the situation was. She took a deep breath and looked around.

A lamp was on the little table by her side, so she switched it on. She could see James sitting on the edge of the bed. The door behind him led to a landing. The door in the corner of the room presumably led into a bathroom or a cupboard. There were no windows except for a large Velux in the angled ceiling. She realised she was in some sort of attic room. She noted that she was fully clothed. At least that was a good sign. She checked to see what the time was but he'd removed her watch from her wrist. She couldn't learn anymore about her predicament until she opened a dialogue with James.

"Where the hell are we?" Her voice came out very gravelly; perhaps she should have risked the glass of water.

"We are somewhere where we can talk without interruption. No Bruce or Libby to barge in. Just the two of us like old times." Charlotte didn't like that 'old times' context. It had connotations of a previous chapter in their lives that was over. She knew she had to keep him talking. She felt lousy but needed to focus on how to get out of there. It was obviously night time, hopefully the same day, she knew people would be worrying about her so she needed to get her head in the right place to deal with the difficult situation.

"What do you want to talk about that hasn't been discussed already?" She needed the toilet but wanted to start a conversation with her captor.

"I need you to understand that I still love you and want us to begin again. We could be happy again, Charlie. Have children and become a family again. I've learned my lesson. Libby was just a fling. She meant nothing to me. You are the one I have always loved." Charlotte had to be careful how she replied. She wanted to get out of there but her impetuous reaction was to tell him he was an egomaniac to think any woman would want him. He only wanted his old life back because he had everything he wanted; a nice house, a job, a wife/ housekeeper/cook/nurse/breadwinner – in other words Charlotte.

"So where do we go from here James?" Something inside her brain told her to keep him talking. She wasn't sure why but whenever she had watched films with kidnappings they always seemed to try and keep the kidnapper talking. The whole situation felt surreal.

"I want you to tell me how you really feel about me. Then we can decide what to do next." James was smiling at her. It sent a shiver down her spine. She could imagine exactly what 'next' meant and it was the last thing she was going to let happen.

"Well James, if I'm totally honest," she stopped herself. Totally honest at that juncture could be fatal. She didn't know what the new James was capable of. "I need the loo." She smiled at him. Perhaps if she acted normally and not scared, it would put him at ease. "You know I have never been able to concentrate on anything when I need the loo." He smiled and pointed to the small door in the corner of the room. She tried to put her feet onto the ground but swayed and grabbed the bedside table. James got up and steadied her. He walked towards the toilet slowly, holding her up. Once they were at the en suite she shut the door on him. Luckily there was a bolt; a lot of use that would be if he wanted to get in. One thrust and it would pull the screws out, no problem. Charlotte straightened up. She did feel a little woozy but nothing like she had given James to believe. She was throwing him off his guard in case she had the opportunity to make a quick get-away. There was a Velux in the en suite. She stood on the toilet. She could just see the horizon on tip-toe. It was dark but she could make out some lights in the distance so people were still awake. She had heard a few trains rumble passed so it couldn't be too late.

"Are you okay Charlie?" James was getting impatient.

"Yes, it's taking a little longer trying to do everything I

need to do. I feel like I'm drunk. I'm sure I only had one glass of wine." She didn't want James to think she was angry with him, or that the situation was anything other than normal. She went to the loo quickly, flushed the toilet and splashed her face with water. Perhaps she could ask him to get her something to eat. That would make him at least leave the room. He may let her go down with him, but she wouldn't hold her breath. She was getting very nervous. The old James was an idiot, but an intelligent idiot. Romantic at the beginning of their relationship and, dare she say loving. The James in front of her had totally freaked her out. He was a different person. A lot of talk recently had been about depression. Bipolar and schizophrenia came to mind, but do people suddenly develop it? She hadn't a clue, but it would explain a lot. She came out of the toilet and found James hovering outside the door. He helped her back into bed. She'd keep the charade up for a while longer.

"Would you like me to help you get more comfortable Charlie?" He started fussing about with her pillows.

"No thank you, I'm fine." She politely pushed his hand away.

"There are some night clothes in the drawer over there and clean underwear." He pointed to the small chest of drawers by the door. "I bought them this morning from a department store I know you use. They are size medium, just to be on the safe side." Charlotte normally would have said something, she was very proud of her petite figure, but it wasn't the time to be offended. He opened the drawer and held up umpteen packets of knickers.

"Oh my God James. How long are you proposing to keep me here?" Bugger, she didn't mean it to come out quite so forceful, but the sight of a couple of weeks of underwear shocked her. She took a deep breath and tried the question again, a little more tactfully. "Are we staying here long?" She had also noted the abundance of women's magazines, crossword and Sudoku books. James had lost his smile and was frowning.

"I thought we'd stay until you saw reason. It's obviously going to take longer than I thought." He got up to leave the room. He turned back to her at the door. "Just remember this, if I can't have you back, Bruce won't get you either." Charlotte was panicking. She didn't know whether this new James was capable of violence. Did he mean he would kill one of them, or both? Quickly she had to defuse the atmosphere.

"I'm hungry." She was actually feeling nauseous but couldn't think of anything else to say. "Have we any food in the house?" That sounded like normal, everyday chat. She tried to keep it going. "I could make you a nice meal, like old times." Play him at his own game, she thought. She smiled as hard as she could. His face wasn't giving anything away. Had he calmed down? He smiled back at her.

"I wouldn't want you to injure yourself coming down the stairs. I'll cook you something tonight, maybe tomorrow you can reciprocate, if you are feeling better." With that he shut the door and she heard the bolt going across.

The whole situation was ridiculous, bizarre even, if it wasn't so sinister. In the frame of mind James was in Charlotte couldn't predict what he was capable of if he didn't get his way. He'd already drugged her, kidnapped her and locked her in a room. He may have a weapon. She got up and turned the ceiling light on, in the hope that illumination would bring ideas of escape into her brain. She looked around the room to no avail. He hadn't even left her handbag, so she had no communication devices. She would just have to wait until an opportunity revealed itself and be ready. She took the glass and emptied it into the basin in the en suite. She was not going to risk it. She then poured a fresh glass from the tap. She drank the whole glass and poured another and continued the pattern glass after glass until she physically couldn't drink any more. She wanted to get any traces of the drug out of her system. She needed all her faculties to get through the nightmare she was in.

Madonna's radio crackled into the silence of the lounge. Everyone sat up and watched as the police officer left the room. She had an earpiece on so they couldn't hear what was being said only her monosyllabic replies. She signed off and went back into the lounge where the men were all on the edge of their seats.

"Any news?" George was trying to keep it together for Bruce and Alan's sake. Who said that men were stronger than women? At that point, she had to disagree.

"Well, they now know where the car is. We have a helicopter up to check out the area. What they don't want to do is spook him. The local bobbies are just waiting for their trained negotiator before they decide on the next course of action. Not wanting to worry you, but we don't know if he's armed."

"We'd rather you told us everything." Bruce couldn't honestly say if James would be armed or not. He had changed beyond recognition in the last few months.

"That's all they could tell me. At least they think they've

found them. That's a good thing this early in the case. The first twenty-four hours are crucial in abductions." Bruce thought he was watching a TV soap. But this was real. He got up and poured Alan and Tom a glass of brandy.

"What about me?" George was trying to stay upbeat and positive for the sake of her father.

"We'll want someone sober in case we need a driver." Bruce was on her wavelength. He'd seen her glance at her dad. Alan was looking greyer by the minute. He looked over to the young police constable. She could do with a stiff drink too, but he knew she would refuse. "So Madonna, any other nicknames at your station worth knowing?" The constable looked thoughtful. Bruce needed to kill some time and try to keep everyone from agonising too much over what was happening to Charlotte. The exasperation at not being able to do anything other than wait was getting to them all.

"None I'd be allowed to tell you. But we have everyday nicknames for certain ranks and support officers." She knew the conversation was slightly inappropriate, but if she could help them keep an eye on reality while their world was upside-down, she'd give it a go. "We call the Community Support Officers plastics". Bruce looked puzzled. "From the blue bands on their caps." Realisation dawned on their faces and they tried to smile. She carried on. "The civvies that help at the station are known as strawberries." She looked round the room to see if anyone could guess why.

"From the old strawberry Mivis, you know, the ice lollies?" Alan smiled. That was his favourite treat from the ice-cream van as a child. Georgina looked around and realised that the officer was helping.

"I'll only tell you a few more if you promise that no one

will ever know where you heard them from." They all nodded. She was pleased that they were all in on the secret. She had got them all out of limbo for a little while. "Okay, this one isn't very nice, so I don't use it myself, but the traffic police are known as black rats. Allegedly it's because black rats are the only animal that eat their own young." That got a reaction from Georgina.

"Yuk. How gross." Tom, on the other hand had been caught speeding on numerous occasions and could see the humour in it.

"My favourite is the electronic tags that go on ankles which are affectionately known as a Peckham Rolex." She liked that one, so did her audience. "I assume from Del Boy and Rodney. I can't remember what the programme's called, but my dad has it on most weekends."

"*Only Fools and Horses*. Good programme that. They don't make them like that anymore, more's the pity." Alan had come out of his torpor.

"God Daddy, that shows your age." George was glad to see her father a little perkier.

"Anyone for another coffee?" Madonna hated the situation these people were in, but she loved her job, especially when she could keep their anxiety at a rational level.

Charlotte could hear a helicopter buzzing about overhead and into the distance. Had they found her? Surely they couldn't have found them there, in the middle of nowhere. When she looked out of the Velux window the only sign of life was in the distance. But she hoped that the helicopter had seen something that had alerted the police. She looked around the room to find something she could hang out of the window in an effort to attract attention when she heard James at the door. She ran back into bed.

James opened the door slowly and checked Charlotte was in the bed. He then reached down and picked up a tray from the landing floor. He placed it on the bedside table. She looked over at it and couldn't decide if it was a bowl of soup or stew. It was accompanied by a piece of French stick that she had already decided was all she could stomach. Liquid was dubious in case he'd drugged it again.

"Looks lovely James." She had to be more careful how she conversed with him. Keeping him amenable could only help the situation.

"It's only from a tin. Not up to your culinary standard, but I haven't met anyone who is." Normally she'd have been flattered by a compliment like that, but not at that moment. He reached up and touched her cheek. She tried not to give away her feeling of abject repulsion. James realised that the softness of Charlie's skin was one of the things that he had fallen for when they got together on their first date. He felt he had a good chance of getting her back, just needed a little more time. He thought she was already mellowing.

Luckily James's touch was gentle. He was behaving like the James she had met and dated at the beginning of their relationship. When did he change? What had changed him? Charlotte knew Libby wasn't the reason he'd left; she was just the answer to his needs. It was her own fault. She had been a workaholic and had lost her husband and daughter because of it. James was misconstruing Charlie's tears. He wiped them away gently. He smiled at her and she smiled back. If she got out of the situation she was in she made a promise to herself that work would have to be secondary in her life. Bruce deserved her undivided attention. He'd been through a bad time too. She needed to make her new romance work or she'd end up a sad, lonely old woman, rich but alone.

She looked up at James. Thank goodness he couldn't read minds. He'd have been furious that all his efforts to woo Charlie back to him were in vain. James's own mixed-up mind had made Charlotte's so clear. She knew exactly what she wanted but she still needed to get out of there alive, unscathed. She'd do what it took even if it took every ounce of compassionate acting.

The helicopter buzzed over the house again. Charlotte couldn't help but look at James to see his reaction.

"Don't worry. It's not for us. We are very near the helicopter pad at the local police headquarters. It comes and goes quite often. Probably out looking for criminals." Charlotte would have laughed if it weren't so ironic. She felt resigned and decided to keep her strength up by at least eating the bread. "I'm just popping down to have the rest of the tin myself. I'll be up with your pudding later. Perhaps we can resume our cosy chat when I get back?" He left her to her supper, locking the door on his way out.

She was actually getting angry now. She was not going to go down the victim road. It was almost over-riding her fear. She put down the tray on the side of the bed and got up, walking towards the door. She tried the handle. Then pulled to see how much resistance there was. Could she open it? If the door opened the other way she could have leant her whole force behind it and it would probably have opened, but not inwards. Knowing that police headquarters was so near made her even angrier. Had he chosen that spot to make her feel even more exasperated? She wouldn't put it past him.

There was a commotion from downstairs. She could hear raised voices. She wondered whether to shout to let the intruders know she was there, then thought better of it. She hadn't a clue where she was or who it could be so she decided to lock herself in the en suite, therefore having a slight advantage if anyone came into the room to do her harm.

Whoever the intruders were, they certainly wanted everyone to know they were there. The banging and crashing was loud. She could hear her bedroom door being unlocked. Then there was a tapping sound on the toilet door. She held her breath.

"Mrs Whitfield can you open the door? This is the police. You are safe to come out now. We have got Mr Whitfield detained. He can't harm you now." Charlotte couldn't believe it was over so easily. She wasn't sure what to do. She heard the muffled sound of a radio and realised it was a police radio. "Please come out Mrs Whitfield, we need to check you are okay." Charlotte opened the door and found a very friendly face attached to a police officer and burst out crying. She felt foolish, but the officer took hold of her and let her cry. He knew it was relief from the ordeal that had opened the floodgates, very normal at the end of these situations, the happy endings anyway.

"You're safe now, it's all over. Let's get you home." Charlotte was helped down the first and second set of stairs. She was in the attic after all. They helped her outside and into a waiting police car. James had been driven off handcuffed so she didn't have to see him. Another police officer was checking James's car and signalled to his partner.

"Oh look, he's found your handbag. I'll get it for you." He handed her the bag and she checked and found her phone was in it. There were quite a few texts and missed calls, mainly from Bruce and George. She did a joint text back to them both.

"I'm on my way home ☺"

CHAPTER 17

Bruce was the first to grab his phone. Georgina wasn't far behind. Bruce sat down on reading it. He gulped and tried to stop the tears of relief in his eyes and passed his phone to Alan.

"She's on her way home, thank goodness." George hugged Tom.

"Well I think my job is nearly done. I'm so glad we had a good result. Anyone want a coffee before I go?" Madonna wanted to get off duty. She was supposed to be home by ten p.m. but was used to working over until a job was finished. She was glad she was able to see this one through though, because she liked happy endings. Georgina wanted to kill time until her sister got home. "I'll do it. Tea or coffee?"

Bruce just wanted to see Charlotte. He felt he had saturated his body enough with fluids for one evening.

Bruce went to the front door and walked down the driveway. Alan joined him.

"I thought we'd lost her, Alan." He was trying to keep it together but felt tears brewing in his eyes. Alan put his arm round Bruce.

"I've been there before, but we forget how much resilience Charlotte has." Bruce nodded, how right he was. "I'm going back in, there's a nip in the air. I may actually enjoy another brandy now. You wait here for her, I'm sure she'll want to see you before any of us!" Alan was pleased for them both. He was happy to see his daughter with a lovely man at last. He walked back up to the house.

With no traffic about they made it back to her house in sixteen minutes. The officer let her out of the car and then fiddled with his radio while Bruce took her off her feet in a huge bear hug. He couldn't talk, tears were pouring down his face. Charlotte was trying to be strong, but after all she'd been through in the last twelve hours she too ended up crying, but for joy. She was in the security of Bruce's arms.

The police driver coughed. "We'll be off then." The officers had to get back to their own area in case they were needed for another job.

"Thank you so much for everything." Charlotte smiled at the officer who had rescued her. He winked at her.

"All in a day's work ma'am. You take care now." She nodded and waved goodbye to her rescuers.

Bruce held her hand and walked her up the driveway. He knew the rest of the family were just as eager to see her. He had so many questions to ask her, but he wanted her back into the safety of her own house and into the arms of her loving family. Questions could come later.

Georgina and Alan wouldn't let her go. They stood in the same spot for ages just hugging each other.

The doorbell rang. PC Catling went to answer the door. With her limited past experience, she knew you often got the press at all hours of the day and night. She'd have to keep them away until the police had got statements so protocol was to delay the family talking to the press. It wasn't the press it was DS Mellowes. He walked in on the scene he liked, a reunited happy family. Bruce noticed him and introduced him to Charlotte.

"This is DS Mellowes, Charlotte. He is the officer who has been leading the investigation." Charlotte shook his hand.

"Thank you DS Mellowes, I can't tell you how grateful I am." Charlotte looked at him with admiration.

"It was a team effort Mrs Whitfield. We are just all glad you are home safely. And please call me Marsh. DS Mellowes is a bit of a mouthful." He grabbed a rogue digestive from the coffee table. He hadn't eaten all evening.

"I've just realised something." Tom was chuckling. "Is that your real first name?" DS Mellowes knew where that line of enquiry was going.

"Yes. And before you all fall about laughing, my parents had a very bad sense of humour. Who else would name their child after a sweet? Marsh Mellowes, for goodness sake. You wouldn't believe how much ribbing I got at school. Probably why I became a policeman." He was used to people finding his name funny. It was a good icebreaker and came in handy in his tension-filled job. Looking at the family it had worked its magic yet again. "I was going to get a statement off you Mrs Whitfield, but it can wait until the morning. I'll be round after breakfast say ten?" Charlotte nodded. That would give her time to look a little more human than she felt at that moment. "Good. Now I'll take Madonna back to the station so she can get off duty. We'll leave you all to get reacquainted." He laughed at his own joke. Tom thought he'd obviously got his sense of humour from his parents. "Just one thing, please do not discuss this ongoing investigation with anyone outside this room. It could jeopardise the prosecution of Mr Whitfield." Nobody wanted James to get off on a technicality, especially if it was their own fault.

They thanked PC Catling for looking after them so well. George wanted to make sure the detective-sergeant heard the accolades so she would get a good appraisal when it was due.

Once the police officers had left, Charlotte briefly outlined her day, keeping the fear and anxiety out of her voice as best she could for the sake of her father and sister.

By the time she had got to the point of locking herself in the toilet, realising the knock on the door was from a friend not foe, Alan was asleep on the settee so Georgina decided to take him home. Tom helped Alan up and they left Bruce and Charlotte to themselves. It was very late, almost two o'clock in the morning and Charlotte had to be interviewed in a few hours' time, so Bruce made her a nice hot chocolate drink and took it up to her bedroom. Charlotte had already gone up and was languishing in a bath, feeling clean for the first time in hours. He put the cocoa on the side of the bath and sat on the toilet with the lid down, just watching her.

"I realised how much I loved you when I thought I'd lost you." Bruce's voice was trembling. Charlotte had only just noticed that Bruce was shaking. It must have been worse for those waiting for news. At least she knew she was alive. She held out her hand and he clasped it.

"I realised how much I loved you when I thought the alternative was staying in a random cottage with James for the rest of my life." She grinned. He grabbed a towel and held it up for her. She stepped out of the bath and he rubbed her down until she was dry. He left her to do whatever else she needed to do before bed and took her cocoa in to the bedroom placing it on her bedside cabinet. That small gesture of letting her have some privacy told Charlotte that he had been brought up to respect women and treat them with dignity, a major failing of her ex. By the time she'd finished drying her hair and cleaning her teeth Bruce was already in the bed. She slid in next to him and they held each other until they both fell asleep, exhausted.

The next morning DS Mellowes arrived to take Charlotte's statement down. Bruce was allowed to stay. They had debated as to whether to call Jeremy, but decided that was a little excessive, especially as she was the victim, not the perpetrator.

"Did he put up much of a fight when your lot arrested him?" Bruce had only heard Charlotte's side of the events leading to his incarceration.

"No that was the funny thing. The local bobbies were waiting for the negotiator when one of them caught sight of Mr Whitfield in the kitchen window wearing rubber gloves. That got them worried in case he'd put them on for a sinister reason. So it was decided not to wait and one of the bobbies just went to the door and knocked. Mr Whitfield answered it and the rest is history. The funny thing was that Mr Whitfield was only doing the washing up."

Charlotte didn't know why but she wanted to know what was happening to James.

"He's in a cell at the police station at the moment, he'll be remanded in custody while he has his mental health assessed then we will be able to decide which secure establishment to take him to. Don't worry, it'll be a long time before he is let out." He assumed her query was for her safety, but even after all James had done, she felt sorry for him. "Right, can we start with your arrival at the restaurant?" Charlotte told the police officer all that she could remember, having a large part of the day before completely blank in her memory. He put her mind at rest.

"We searched Mr Whitfield's flat and found Rohypnol tablets on a table. Two were missing from the pack. There was an amateur pestle and mortar, a ramekin dish and the back of a dessertspoon, where we could see the remnants of powder. So it isn't rocket science to understand what he'd done. To reinforce the proof of drugging, we found more evidence on his computer, still on the Google page, with the instructions on how to drug someone with Rohypnol." For a computer geek, DS Mellowes thought James was an idiot not to wipe it all clean before he left to carry out the deed. "On another tab on the computer was information of the cottage he had rented through the Airbnb website. Basically, he's bang to rights." He liked saying that.

"So, do you need Charlotte to have a blood test to have proof that he had administered the drug?" Bruce needed to make sure there was no loophole a good solicitor could get James off on.

"No point. That is the tricky thing about Rohypnol. It doesn't stay in the system very long. By now there'd probably be no trace of it. Don't worry, with all the evidence we already have there's no need for Mrs Whitfield to go through any more distress." He got up and straightened all his papers into a folder. "I'll leave you both to the rest of your life. Have a good one." He shook Bruce's hand while Charlotte went to open the front door.

"Thank you and please thank everyone who helped find me." She shook his hand and he left, gratified that his and his team's hard work had been appreciated.

She was about to close the door when she saw her car being driven up the driveway. She went outside to see Tom driving it. Georgina followed in her car.

"Hello Charlie. We decided the last thing you needed was to return to the scene of the crime, so we thought we'd surprise you." Georgina gave her sister a hug.

"You are the best, you two. Thank you." They were right. It was a little too soon to go back to Pizzeria Roma. Tom joined them on the doorstep. "How did you get it here. Don't tell me you hotwired it Tom, or you may end up in a cell next to James." He handed her the keys.

"I got them off Bruce last night. I don't know what to do with this though." He handed her a parking ticket. She didn't know why, but she burst out laughing. Bruce came out to see what was going on. He looked puzzled.

"What's she laughing at Tom?" George and Charlotte had walked into the house, both finding it amusing.

"I handed her a parking ticket. Can't see the funny side, but I'm sure it must be a girl thing." Bruce slapped Tom on the back.

“Thanks for bringing the car back, mate. Another hurdle got over with the most unexpected result. I’m sure they’ll share the joke, eventually.” They joined the girls in the kitchen.

“Oh my darling Bruce, after the worst ordeal of my life, all I have to show for it is a bloody parking ticket. It certainly grounds you that’s for sure. Right you lot it isn’t a holiday. Let’s get back to work. George, I need to hear what the result of our meeting with the publisher was. Bruce, you need to check back with the accountants to make sure they have all the information they need for the VAT people. Tom, what are you doing here getting in the way of the wheels of industry? Haven’t you got a plane that needs guiding in?” Charlotte was back in control and they loved it.

During the course of the next few months’ things settled down. James had been assessed and was put into a secure mental unit after being diagnosed with bipolar disorder, with the hope that with medication and therapy he could eventually be released. Charlotte and Bruce’s divorces were finalised. The business had evolved to the point that they had to employ five more members of staff. Charlotte and Bruce had found office premises above a town centre beauty salon. The rent was low because it had no street access. Luckily their business didn’t rely on passing trade so it wasn’t a problem. Bruce had moved in with Charlotte on a permanent basis and they had settled into a happy comfortable relationship. They spent Christmas at Alan’s, the girls’ family home and Georgina and Tom and Alan joined them for Hogmanay in Scotland where they were officiated into the Gordon clan with open arms.

Spring was on its way and life was getting back to normal.

Bruce went downstairs first, as was his habit. He liked to get the pancakes ready for Charlotte. He noticed the post on the doormat. One caught his eye. It was franked with Angus Council on the top. If it was good news he'd tell Charlotte immediately, if bad he would wait until the wine bottle was open that evening. He went into the kitchen and opened it. He whooped very loudly.

"Have you won £25 on the Premium Bonds?" Charlotte heard his delight from the stairs.

"No, something even better. Our plans have been passed for our 'wee hoose'." He spun here round in a jig. "We can start building as soon as we want." Charlotte was happy, mainly because Bruce was ecstatic. He had longed for Libby to love Scotland and have frequent visits there. After all there were so many flights to choose from, it was hardly a long way away. But he could never share his Scotland with her. On the other hand, he was convinced that Charlotte loved Scotland almost as if she had been born there.

"We better go up at the weekend to talk to the architect then." Charlotte wanted Bruce to have his wee hoose; he deserved it.

"Well as long as you square it with my boss." He looked at her cheekily. He'll never tire of saying it, even if they were equal in the business. He liked winding her up.

Charlotte sorted through the rest of the post and was intrigued by a pink envelope addressed to Mrs C. Whitfield and Mr B. Gordon. She showed it to Bruce with one eyebrow up.

"If you open it you'll know who it's from." He joked. But she was a little apprehensive.

"Surely you recognise the writing, Bruce." She held it to his face again. The smile left his face. "You open it, see what she wants." Bruce took it from her and opened the envelope from his ex-wife.

Dear Charlotte and Bruce,

Long time no see! I am inviting you both to a dinner party for you to meet my veterinarian boyfriend Joshua. I hope you both can come. Details on attached card.

Lots of love, as always

Libby

Still inside the envelope was an embossed card with their names on and the date and time of the dinner party. They were both at a loss for words.

"Do you want to go?" Bruce was happy either way. He knew their relationship was so strong that it could weather any storm, even Libby's tsunami tendencies. Charlotte needed more time to think.

"I want to say no. But have I punished her enough by stealing the best person she ever had in her life from right under her nose?" Bruce looked chuffed. God, he was so edible, she knew she would have to stop flirting with him or she'd get no work done. "I'll think about it during today. I know she's sorry and considering the outcome I'm sure James was the instigator, but I still feel betrayed." Bruce put his arm around her.

"I will go with your decision, but what you have to determine is will you feel happier having your old friend back in your life or ignoring her forever." He was right. She didn't feel very happy ignoring Libby. She had missed her, although she wouldn't admit it. Maybe with time she could build up a relationship bordering on friendship with her ex best friend.

"I'm so happy I've got a clever boyfriend." She kissed him affectionately. "Now I must get some work done today. If you get on with the pancakes I'll make the coffee. What a team we make!" They let go of each other and got on with the task of making breakfast.

Bruce had gone to check the office personnel were all present and correct while Charlotte perused her emails. A message pinged onto her screen from George. It made Charlotte laugh. She hadn't seen so many exclamation marks in a message as the one in front of her.

"OMG!!!! Got an invite from Libby this morning in the post!! For dinner!! What is that woman on??!!!! And she has a new boyfriend!!!! A vet!!!!! I thought they were supposed to be intelligent!!!! Obviously the reason for the invitation is to show off that she's got a boyfriend with an -ology (as Mummy would say!) Do we care?!!!!!!! Did you get one? ☹"

George sounded angry. Charlotte thought about it and realised she wasn't angry. She was actually pleased for Libby. She replied to George's message.

"Hello darling sister. In answer to your first question, yes, we received an invitation. In answer to your second question, yes, I think we will go. ☺"

She waited for George's reply. Within seconds she got the reply.

"!!!!!!!!!!!!!!!!!!!!"

Charlotte wanted to finish her emails so decided she'd call George later. Hopefully George would come round once the shock of getting the invitation had gone. The more Charlotte thought about it the more she knew she was doing the right thing. She also knew for Bruce's sake that it would be nice for him to see Libby settled and happy.

Bruce went home for lunch. He found Charlotte on the internet booking flights for the weekend up to Scotland. He kissed her neck.

"Bruce, I need to finish this before I'm timed out." She loved him being playful. "If you want to be useful, take the sausages out of the oven and cut some French stick." She just needed her security code and she was finished. "There, all done. We have an appointment with your dad's builder friend at the site after we've seen the architect. It's rather exciting, isn't it?" She got off the stool and grabbed Bruce for a cuddle.

Bruce cuddled her back with the oven mitts still on his hands. He loved the domesticity that surrounded their life. He wanted to marry Charlotte so badly, but she had been so hurt. He knew time would heal, but he was impatient. One day soon he'd ask her. He was sure the right moment would show itself.

Charlotte showed Bruce George's message while they were eating their lunch. He found the exclamation marks amusing but the prose a little worrying.

"Have you spoken to her? She sounds angry." Charlotte shook her head.

"I messaged her back to say we were going, but I haven't heard anymore from her. I was going to call her when I had a moment."

"So, you have decided we're going?" Charlotte nodded. Bruce smiled. "I think you have made a good decision. I'm really proud of you Charlotte. That took some balls. Well done old girl." She looked up and looked into Bruce's eyes. From anyone else it could have sounded patronising, but Bruce meant it from his heart. She smiled at him.

"Now the problem will be what to wear." Charlotte tried to make it sound like she was confident in her decision by resorting to humour. Bruce saw through it.

"You'll look lovely in anything. Stop worrying about it. Ring your sister and get her to come too. I have to admit I'm a little curious to see who this chap is who's taken on such a nightmare. Perhaps we should warn him." Bruce was tongue in cheek.

"Don't you dare! If it means you have Libby off your hands once and for all, he has my vote." Just as they were clearing lunch away Charlotte's mobile rang. She picked it up and answered it.

"I've been thinking, perhaps we need to give Libby a second chance at being our friend. She cocked it up the first time, big time, but I think she'll have learned from her mistake." George had had a few hours to calm down and think.

"You're also are dying to see what this vet is like." Charlotte knew her sister better than anyone, because they were very alike.

"Okay, that might have swayed me a little." George had to admit she was intrigued. *"So, what are you going to wear?"* Charlotte burst out laughing. *"What's so funny?"*

"That's just what I've been discussing with Bruce, how funny. Well we've got a week to find something. We're off to Scotland this weekend. The planning permission came through so we need to get on and build our 'wee hoose' as soon as we can. I'll let you decorate your room. It's so beautiful up there George, we're going to love spending time with Bruce's family and there's plenty of room for Daddy at Bella's too. She and Johnny think he's braw for a Sassenach!" Charlotte had tried to put on a Scottish accent. The girls were laughing at the attempt. Bruce was listening and felt contented. He smiled at Charlotte and left the sisters chatting while he went off to organise the finance for their new project.

CHAPTER 18

~~~

The trip to Scotland was short but jam-packed. Bruce's family came from all parts to see them both. Charlotte was a hit with them all, unlike that 'prima donna' as Helen called Libby.

They had briefly been given a summary of the ordeal Charlotte had been through. What came out of it in Bella's eyes was that her son was truly in love with Charlotte.

Bruce wanted as little disturbance to his parents as possible, so the first item on the agenda was to make a separate driveway for all the vehicles to enter the plot. They had staked out the boundary before they left and Johnny was happy that he didn't have to tend that side of the land ever again. It had halved his workload and gave him more time to play golf. Well, that was what he thought, but Bella had other ideas!
~~~

On their return Charlotte wasn't feeling too good. Bruce put it down to all the rushing around.

"It's probably jetlag!" Charlotte joked.

"Doctor's orders, please take it easy this week until you feel better. The business can run itself and I need you. My best shirt needs washing for the monumental dinner party at the end of the week." He was laughing. Charlotte tried to look cross, but ended up laughing with him.

"I have no plans this week apart from shopping with George for a frock. As Libby's chief cook and bottle-washer will be a guest this time, I wonder who will be doing the cooking?" Charlotte wondered if that was the attraction of Libby's new vet. "If the truth be known, I am quite looking forward to meeting the Adonis who has finally trapped the Diva." Bruce nodded.

"I think it will be a very interesting night." He winked at her and gave her a hug. "Now remember, shopping and lunch, but no work today, promise?" Charlotte loved the way Bruce looked after her. She promised.

Georgina picked Charlotte up to go shopping to find them both something to wear at the weekend. As they entered their local department store George had a thought.

"Do we go over-the-top or play it subtle?" George wanted to go with whatever Charlie decided. Charlotte thought about it.

"It's our first meeting with her new beau. It'll be better if we play it down otherwise he'll think we are showing off. We know Libby will be dressed to the nines, but I think we will look classier in pretty, casual dresses rather than silk, diamonds and tiaras for a dinner party!" George burst out laughing.

"I've just pictured Libby in gloves and a puffy ball gown with structured undergarments!" They were both laughing so loudly that the customers on the Ladies' Fashion floor were staring at them.

They both managed to choose dresses that complemented their small figures and also looked elegant and sophisticated. Charlotte had a voucher for 20% off from a previous purchase so they decided to splurge their savings on a fish lunch at the famous restaurant on the beach.

It was a sunny day and from their table they could see the Isle of Wight on one side and Old Harry Rocks on the other. The sea looked calm and beautiful. Both girls sat back and took in the view. Charlotte was still feeling a little queasy so decided to have just water rather than a glass of the house white.

"You ok, sister dear? Not like you to refuse wine." George looked at her sister and knew there was something wrong. "You look tired. I hope you aren't coming down with anything. Tom and I will not go to the dinner party without you and Bruce, that's for certain." She smiled at Charlotte. Nobody talked about the kidnapping, but George wondered if Charlie should have had some counselling after it. Delayed shock and post-traumatic stress syndrome were not conditions to be taken lightly. She'd have a word with Bruce when they were alone at the office.

"Don't be daft. I'm not going down with anything. I'm just having an off day. I told Bruce this morning that I thought it was jetlag." George still looked worried. "I woke up feeling sick, and it hasn't subsided yet, that's all." George raised an eyebrow.

"Have you had that feeling before? Feeling sick all

morning? Or putting it another way, morning sickness?" Charlotte suddenly realised what George was getting at. It had crossed her mind that the feelings were similar to what George was hinting at.

"I'll pop into the chemist on our way home and get a test. Now can we enjoy our lunch? I can just about stomach steamed cod, but perhaps not fried in batter." They both settled down to their lunch, excited at the prospect of the result later that day.

On their way home George parked outside the chemist while Charlotte dashed in. She bought two tests, just in case. She returned to the car and told George to get a move on.

"I can't believe how excited I am at the prospect of having Bruce's baby. If I am pregnant I hope Bruce will be just as pleased." Charlotte fiddled with the boxes.

"Are you blind or stupid? That man adores you. He has done since James buggered off. He would do anything for you. Do you want me to spell it out for you? Charlie, he loves you." George looked over at her sister and saw tears running down her face. She didn't mean to shout at her. But then Charlotte looked up and there was a broad grin on her face.

"He does, doesn't he?" She wiped her eyes and swore at the traffic lights as they turned red.

They pulled up outside Charlotte's house and she ran in as quickly as she could, pulling open one of the boxes as she went. George walked in after her and wondered whether to put the kettle on. Her mother would have. Good or bad news you needed a nice cup of tea. She decided to put the kettle on. Charlie walked out of the downstairs toilet with the stick in her hand.

"This feels like déjà vu. Can you look?" She handed the stick to her sister.

"For best results, you should really do this first thing in the morning." George looked at her sister's impatient face. "Or now is a perfect time." She smiled at Charlotte. Charlotte busied herself taking over the making of the tea, glancing at her sister every five to ten seconds in case her face gave anything away.

"Eureka!! Charlotte you are having a baby!" George thrust the stick into Charlotte's hand and grabbed her tightly, squeezing her and jumping at the same time. Charlotte joined in jumping in unison with George. They were both so happy. They stopped when Charlotte's phoned pinged with a new message. It was Bruce asking her if she'd had a lovely day with her sister and if she was feeling better.

"I am so tempted to tell him George, but after my last pregnancy I think I'd like to wait until I've been to the doctor." After the initial excitement had died down Charlotte remembered her miscarriage.

"This time you will have no stress; you will be looked after by the most generous, amazing Scotsman this side of Hadrian's Wall. The business is running itself, almost. So, you just have to relax, be healthy and enjoy the experience." George wasn't looking as happy as earlier. It brought it home to her that now she had given up teaching, she and Tom would love a baby. They had been trying for months with no joy. But this was her sister's moment. She would be happy for Charlotte. Anyway, she and Tom were enjoying the practise. They drank their tea and just as George was about to leave, Charlotte handed her the spare pregnancy test.

"Keep it, hopefully you'll need it soon." Charlotte wasn't stupid. She had noticed the longing in George's eyes when she read the result. They hugged each other. "By the way, don't tell Tom. He and Bruce gossip more than us!" George knew that was true. If they could sneak recording devices into their men's golf bags they'd have enough gossip to write a novel on just the first nine holes, with the sequel on the back nine. "Mum's the word!"

Charlotte and George were upstairs in Charlotte's bedroom. The men were downstairs enjoying a nice bottle of Quinta de Crasto, originally from Portugal, but helpfully sold at the local wine warehouse. Tom had recommended it. It was one of Tom's favourite wines after a visit to the Algarve on a lad's golf weekend a few years earlier. Bruce wasn't allowed to go, Libby didn't trust him. True irony.

"Excellent wine, Bruce, although I say so myself. I hope you have another bottle, you're going to need it tonight!" Tom was right. Bruce was putting on his usual cheerful, laidback face, but inside his stomach was churning. Funnily enough he was more apprehensive for Charlotte than himself.

"Well this evening can go one of two ways." He held up his wine glass to Tom. "Here's to the more pleasant result." They chinked their glasses.

Charlotte heard the glasses clash from upstairs. "The boys are enjoying themselves. Let's hope that carries on throughout the night." George nodded in agreement. She'd just finished curling Charlotte's hair with the tongs. She finished it off with a small silver clip, which had a smattering of diamantés around the edge. Not at all brash, but delicate and tasteful. It belonged to their mother who was one of the most graceful and beautiful women they had known.

"You look just like Mummy." George kissed her sister on the cheek. She noticed Charlotte's cheek was moist with tears. "Sorry darling. I didn't mean to make you sad."

"I'm not sad. It's my hormones! I was thinking the same as you just before you said it. I do miss her George, but I know she is with us all the time." The sisters hugged each other.

Bruce was getting anxious. He had booked the taxi for a quarter to eight and there was no sign of the girls. He went to the bottom of the stairs.

"Hey, you two, are you ready yet?" He didn't want to sound agitated so added, "Your wine is getting drunk." It had the desired effect. He could hear movement and giggling.

"I do love that man." Charlotte sighed while George adjusted her sister's smeared makeup. Luckily the mascara was waterproof but the powder on her cheeks needed replenishing.

"How he hasn't cottoned on to the fact you are pregnant I can't understand. You are positively glowing." George finished the cheeks with a quick flick of the brush.

"I nearly gave it away earlier when he asked what time to book the taxi. Obviously I'm not drinking now, but I stopped myself telling him I'll drive." Was she doing the right thing holding the news from him? What if the same thing happened again? But as George said, the circumstances are totally different. The main one being that she knows she's pregnant and can take the necessary steps to protect her unborn baby. "Come on, let's join the boys. I have to say they are in for a treat when they see their partners for the evening." They linked arms and walked rather ceremoniously down the stairs in their unassuming finery.

"Tom come and look at these two bonny lassies. They have fair taken my breath away." Tom came out of the lounge to join Bruce at the bottom of the stairs.

"Wow you two, you do scrub up well! Only kidding. All I can say is look out Libby, our girls mean business!" The four of them couldn't stop laughing. Just as the girls reached the bottom step the doorbell rang.

"Immaculate timing, as usual, Boss." Charlotte flicked him with her pashmina, but couldn't help smiling as he took her from her sister's arm and steered her to the door. Charlotte was surprised that they were all in such good humour. It did bode well for a lovely evening.

CHAPTER 19

~

As they walked up Bruce's old driveway he stopped.

"Can anyone else hear that?" They all stopped to listen.

"It sounds like a dog barking, coming from inside the house." Tom was the first to state the obvious.

"That's what I thought, but Libby wouldn't have an animal in the house unless it was cooked." Bruce laughed at his own wit. "And we're not in China so I'm sure the dog isn't on the menu; interesting." His eyebrow had taken off. Charlotte was laughing. Perhaps Libby had changed more than they had realised? They'll know in a moment, she thought.

Tom reached the door first and rang the bell. A big dog was jumping up and down excitedly at the front door. From behind they heard a very clipped, well-spoken man's voice telling the animal to behave. The dog immediately stopped.

"I wonder if he's got Libby as well-trained yet." Bruce couldn't resist speaking his thoughts out loud. As the door opened, Charlotte jabbed Bruce and gave him a 'behave' look.

"Good Evening. I am Joshua, Elizabeth is in the kitchen, and she'll be out in a jiffy. Please come in." The 'Adonis' was short, dumpy and had a distinct recession going on in the hair department. He was wearing beige Chinos and a blue and white striped Ralph Lauren shirt. So not Libby's type at all, Charlotte had to admit. The Libby she had known would not have a gentleman at the dinner table without a tie. This man was as casual as if they were off to Waitrose for the weekly groceries, in Libby's old world. Bruce had already spotted the Rolex and knew why Libby had found him attractive. He was the first to move forward and shake his hand.

"Hello there. I'm Bruce of the Glen." Charlotte sighed. If that was the way Bruce coped, with humour, who was she to knock it? She smiled at him giving her approval. Bruce carried on with impunity. "And who's that little fellow?" Bruce pointed to the chocolate Labrador at Joshua's feet.

"This is Rolo. Say hello to Bruce, Rolo." Rolo put up a paw for Bruce to shake. After Bruce's comment about training, Charlotte had to smile, imagining Libby putting her claws forward for Bruce to shake!

Joshua walked over to Charlotte. "You must be Charlotte. Elizabeth described you admirably. How do you do?"

"I'm very well, thank you." Well he had impeccable manners she couldn't fault that.

"And the avid reader, Georgina. How do you do?" George wasn't sure that it was a compliment, but decided to take it as one.

"I'm also very well, thank you." The girls stared at each other both keeping their opinions to themselves, but obviously on the same page.

"And process of elimination, you must be Thomas." Pompous ass, thought Tom. But he'd give him the benefit of the doubt until he knew him better.

"Hi Josh, nice to meet you." In a very steady voice his host replied;

"It's Joshua actually. Now please all go through to the sitting room. You all know where it is." He winked at Bruce, which made Bruce cringe. "While I let Elizabeth know you are here." He left them and went off to the kitchen. There was so much they wanted to say, but good manners and the vicinity of the kitchen stopped them. Facial expressions were in overdrive though.

The Labrador, Rolo, had taken a liking to Bruce and sat leaning up against his leg. Bruce bent down and patted him, missing Libby's entrance. Charlotte and George looked at each other and decided for the first time ever, they were slightly overdressed. Libby was wearing leggings, with a floppy jumper over. Charlotte's first thought was that she looked very outdoorsy.

"Hello everyone. Thank you for coming. I see you have met Joshua and our little boy, Rolo." She bent down and called the dog over. "Come to Mummy then, who's a good boy?" Rolo left Bruce and wagged his tail as he loped over to Libby. She bent down and tickled him behind his ear. Bruce and Charlotte both had their mouths open at the scene in front of them Never in a month of Sunday's would the old Libby even allow a dog in the house, let alone be a 'mummy' to one! "Joshua would you open the wine please. Red everyone? It's a rather good claret. Joshua is a bit of a connoisseur actually, aren't you darling?" He nodded smiling at the adulation his girlfriend had bestowed on him. Tom stopped himself repeating his first impression of the boyfriend, but decided he had to think it or his brain would hurt all night 'pompous ass'!

Charlotte accepted the glass of wine. Libby had been staring at her so she didn't want to give the game away. Apart from her sister, Libby was the only other person who knew her so well and would guess by the smallest gesture that she was pregnant.

"Now, if you all get comfortable, dinner will be ready to serve in ten minutes. I'll leave Joshua to entertain you." The joy, thought Tom. Libby kissed her new man on the cheek and went off to the kitchen.

"So, Joshua, is Libby cooking the dinner?" Bruce wondered if she had help in the kitchen.

"Of course. She is a wonderful cook. It's actually how we met." All enquiring eyes were on Joshua. He put them out of their misery. "Elizabeth was at an intense evening course learning cordon bleu cooking every week night for three months and was in the advanced class by the time I met her. I was called in just before their final exams to help them complement their menus with the right wines. It's my hobby and helps me relax after a busy week healing animals. As a senior partner, I can juggle my hours to fit in with the college curriculum." Tom was finding it difficult not to hit the pompous ass, but found it easier just to call him a pompous prick instead, suited him much better anyway. The girls were looking at Bruce. He'd been stroking Rolo the whole time, but from their angle they could see him laughing into the dog's neck. It made things very difficult for them because Joshua was totally focussed on the two girls. Charlotte didn't want Joshua to think them rude so acted interested.

"So Joshua, you met at cookery classes?"

"Far from it Charlotte. Cordon bleu cuisine is an art. Anyone can cook. Elizabeth got top marks for all her pieces and can be employed in any Michelin star restaurant in the country if she wanted. Obviously, she has no need to work, but I have the benefit of delightful fare every evening, and you lucky people are about to sample it tonight." He looked so proud of his girlfriend. "We met after the lecture on wine. I'm afraid it was love at first sight for me. Elizabeth was putting all her equipment away..." Bruce made a strangulated sound as he was trying too hard to keep a laugh inside.

"Sorry, I was stifling a sneeze, he must be moulting." He pointed at Rolo hoping he had sounded sincere.

"I took the bull by the horns and asked her if she'd like to join me in a nice glass of Malbec at the wine bar opposite the college. She agreed and as the saying goes, the rest is history."

"Ah, how romantic. I wish Tom had swept me off my feet like that. Oh, hang on, he did!" George winked over at her husband. He'd been too quiet and she knew him well enough to know he was bored.

Suddenly a hand-bell rang from the kitchen.

"That's our cue to go through to the dining room. Don't

worry about bringing your glasses. We will be having white wine for the starter so obviously the appropriate glasses will be on the table." Obviously, thought Tom. After all, most pompous pricks would use ten glasses where one would do with a piece of kitchen roll. Joshua led the way into the dining room, turning before he left he pointed at Rolo. "Rolo, stay. I'm sure you don't want a dog in the dining area." Bruce bit his lip; Libby was staying in the kitchen then? He reproached himself immediately, people can change, even Libby.

The dining table was laid out beautifully. The linen napkins were rolled into pretty rose shaped serviette rings. The china service had changed, since Bruce lived there, to a delicate bone china in white with a gold band round the edge, and red and yellow roses on the borders.

"How beautiful. Is that Royal Albert china? It looks very like Mummy's set, doesn't it Charlie?" George loved bone china. Especially when drinking a cup of tea. The delicacy of the thinness on her lips reminded her of her childhood. She dared pick up a side plate and turned it over. She was right. "It is Charlie, Old Country Roses from the Royal Albert collection. I can't believe you have a whole set. We ended up with such a mixture of a few cups, saucers and a couple of plates. They were our grandmother's to start with. Ooh, and a tea pot." Joshua looked very smug.

"My mother left the whole set to me. She knew I would look after it. They have never been in a dishwasher. I find that ruins the best china. Right if you look carefully you will find your places. I shall go and help Elizabeth." Bruce was beginning to resent being there after all. It seemed to him that the whole evening was a show, directed, produced and performed by the vet and the cordon bleu Fanny Cradock.

"Come on Bruce, you are next to me." George had found the embossed cards with their names on tucked into each serviette ring. She ushered him to his seat. George was one side of him and Libby at the end of the table. That meant Charlotte was next to Tom and Joshua at the other end of the table, Bruce's old seat. He sat down and looked at Charlotte. She smiled at him.

"Only a few more hours to go," she grinned. He had to smile. If Charlotte could put up with it so could he.

"I wonder if Daddy still has our Royal Albert collection, Charlie. Shotgun he leaves it to me in the Will." Charlotte had seen the remains of the set recently and apart from a cup and a small plate, the rest had chips and crazing in the glaze. Obviously has been in a dishwasher!

"I'll tell him to pop to the solicitors in the morning and put a codicil on his Will. OK?" They were both enjoying themselves, even if the men were not.

Joshua came back with a bottle of white wine. He had put three glasses at every place and began pouring the wine into one of the glasses and telling his audience all about it.

"This is a Viognier vin, Pays d'Oc from Languedoc. I shall let you all taste it and I hope you get as much enjoyment from the natural aromatics as I do. You may note peach, pear and even violets come through if it has been bottled correctly and hasn't been exposed to too much oxygen. Enjoy." He finished pouring the wine and sat down. They all sipped the wine and nodded towards the host with knowing appreciation. He was pleased. He hadn't wanted to waste it on philistines. Luckily Libby wasn't there to see their charade. She would have sussed it immediately. Another little ring came from the kitchen. "Please excuse me, I think I'm wanted." He moved swiftly to the kitchen.

"Did you see his tail wagging as he left?" Tom had finally had enough.

"Tom! Behave. Actually, I did!" George and the rest of them were laughing when Libby came in with three plates, followed by Joshua with the other three. They were placed in front of everyone and Bruce's stomach rumbled. George had heard it and felt sorry for him. If that was the starter, goodness knows how a grown man was going to have his fill with the rest. On the plate was a beautifully presented scallop, on a bed of a couple of slices of beetroot with a few asparagus spears and on top of the scallop was some cream and a sprinkling of crushed nuts.

"Here we have a seared scallop with Thai asparagus, beetroot carpaccio and hazelnut cream. *Bon appétit.*" Joshua looked over at Libby and put his thumb up nodding. She giggled in a very worrying way. The whole evening was quite bizarre and Charlotte knew about bizarre. Two seconds later the men had finished their first course and felt just as hungry as when they arrived. Bruce thought he'd better speak to his ex-wife.

"Well Libby that was amazing. I'm impressed. If the starter was that good, well I can only imagine how wonderful the rest of the meal is going to be." Charlotte and George nodded in agreement. Tom did not.

"Oh, bless you Bruce. That wasn't the starter. That was just a little amuse-bouche to whet your appetites." She was smiling at him rather condescendingly. It annoyed Tom that the bitch could still hurt his friend.

"My bouche has been amused all evening so far. How about yours, Josh?" George cringed. Tom was out for a fight and she hoped he wasn't going to get one. She didn't blame him at all. In fact, she thought he'd been very restrained up to that moment. He was one of the most loyal friends you could have. He couldn't imagine why they had agreed to an evening in the company of the 'husband stealer' and her pompous prick of a boyfriend, but went with the flow as he always did, but he didn't have to like it. Libby started collecting the plates up while Joshua answered his guest.

"My parents spent months deciding on what to call their first son, so I would like you to respect their choice please, Thomas. I was Christened Joshua so that is my name. Can I refill your glass?" Joshua smiled down at Tom, holding the bottle to his glass. Tom just nodded. Joshua filled all the glasses and then talked to the girls about the business of publishing, until the inevitable ring of the bell.

Bruce had managed to zone out. He was looking around the dining room to see what had changed since he was in residence. Decoration-wise nothing had been altered. Furniture-wise, there didn't seem to be much left that he recognised. There was a hefty sideboard behind Charlotte and Tom that looked antique. It was covered in decanters, glasses of all shapes, sizes and colours, and a couple of bottles of port, brandy and another liqueur that he couldn't see the name of. Joshua had obviously settled in very comfortably and Bruce felt nothing at all. He wasn't jealous, cross, resentful or bitter. He had the best life with a woman who he was deeply in love with. His past was his mistake, his future was a fortunate stoke of karma.

Libby walked in with a further three plates followed by Joshua with the other three. That looked better, Bruce's stomach agreed with him. With the plates placed in front of all the guests Joshua went round topping-up the glasses again. George had managed surreptitiously to swap her empty glass with her sister and finished the second with no problem.

"I shall continue with this wine as it complements any fish jolly well. I can see you like it Charlotte. It is very delicate, just right for the female taste." Oh my God, thought George, what a chauvinistic pig. She knew she wouldn't have been able to tell the difference even if it was cheap plonk from Asda. She had to bite her tongue; she didn't want to draw attention to the fact that Charlotte hadn't even tasted it.

"Here we have tempura prawns with a chilli dip. The dip isn't hot, just tangy. Enjoy. *Bon appétit.*" They were obviously home-made and looked amazing. Charlotte was actually in awe of her ex-best-friend. She decided to be positive and call her a friend for now. "By the way, don't stand on ceremony. The best way to eat these is by hand." She smiled around the table catching Joshua's attention. He smiled back at her and gestured with another thumbs-up. Tom wanted to be sick, but was too hungry to waste anything put in front of him.

Conversation became very stilted so there were a lot of 'yums' and 'mmmms' from the girls. The boys were too busy trying to get as much out of the prawn tails by sucking as hard as they could. Not a pretty sight. But it made the girls laugh.

The plates were taken away and Joshua took the white

wine glasses from the table. He then brought out a bottle of red wine.

"Meat next then?" Tom was sure he knew almost as much as Joshua about wine, but didn't like to brag. George caught his attention and gave him a withering teacher glance. Tom grinned like a naughty schoolboy.

If Charlotte was honest the food was amazing and they were actually having a lovely time, despite Joshua and Libby.

Joshua then droned on about the Southern Rhône region of France where the next wine had come from called Châteauneuf-du-Pape. Although extremely interesting, Bruce wished he'd just get on and pour it instead of sticking his nose down the neck of the bottle and wafting his hand in the air. Tom on the other hand was thinking that Joshua must be worth a bob or two as the wines he was serving weren't cheap. Right on cue the little bell rang from the kitchen and Joshua excused himself.

"It's like being in a restaurant." George exclaimed. "Except we have to sit with the staff!" Once again Libby and Joshua entered the dining room to meet laughter from their guests. She had measured from the mood of her visitors that they were all having a lovely time. It pleased her as she had spent a long time deciding on the menu, knowing their likes and dislikes. She hoped they were enjoying the food and the company. But then who wouldn't enjoy Joshua's company, he was so intelligent and humorous. Again they each had three plates and put them in front of each person.

"Here we have grilled lamb tenderloin, with rosemary sauce, potato gratin and sautéed spinach. I have given you the edges Bruce, as I know you prefer it cooked a little more than the others. *Bon appétit*." Bruce felt honoured. He liked meat red, but not oozing blood like most chefs preferred to serve it.

"Now you can understand why I had chosen this wine." Tom looked at him blankly. "Because it is one of the best wines to compliment lamb." Der! thought Tom, how patronising can this man get. If he had to sit at a table with this vet again, he would have to have a lobotomy first. Then all he'd hear would be blah, blah, blah, blah; so much more entertaining than the drivel that was coming from that end of the table.

The plates were clean and everyone praised Libby for such an amazing meal. Bruce wondered why he hadn't thought of a cookery course for her while they were husband and wife. It would have made his life easier. He much preferred sharing the cooking like he did with Charlotte. Especially in a small kitchen where they had to dance past each other on numerous occasions, which sometimes took longer than necessary.

"I hope you are all enjoying yourselves. I have to admit I was slightly trepidatious about tonight. But it seems my angst was unfounded. I'm so happy you have come to help us celebrate tonight." Joshua had raised himself from the table. He was staring at Libby. Charlotte looked over at Bruce who shrugged his shoulders. Neither had a clue as to what was being celebrated; surely not their friendships back on track? Joshua went over to Libby. He went down on one knee and took her hand. The one thing that Charlotte noticed was that Libby's finger nails were of a short length and had not been covered in a garish varnish. The first time she had seen her with plain nails since they'd left school.

"Elizabeth, I think you are the most wonderful woman in the world. Will you please do me the honour of becoming my wife?" Libby was positively beaming. She was fit to burst with excitement.

"Oh yes please, Joshua. I'd love to." She stood up into his embrace and they kissed passionately. Tom thought it repulsive at the dinner table, so unhygienic, but he was grinning at George. He picked up his glass and held it up.

"Congratulations to you both." He chinked his glass with Bruce.

"No, no." Joshua let go of Libby and rushed over to the sideboard. He took out an ice bucket already filled with ice and a bottle of champagne.

Oh, bloody hell. Are we now going to have a lecture on the Champagne region of France? Tom realised he was being a little childish. After all it was a lovely gesture on Joshua's part and how nice he wanted to share the occasion with total strangers. Another thought entered his head that maybe he hadn't any other friends, but immediately left it as he was trying to be nice.

The flutes from the sideboard were charged and they all toasted the happy couple. Charlotte managed a few sips and was glad that no one was watching her as she took George's empty glass and gave her the full one. George winked at her sister, but realised if she didn't stop drinking for two she'd be on the floor before dessert.

There was a choice of desserts all mouth-wateringly sensational. Libby took the accolades from her guests with relish. They adjourned back into the sitting room much to the delight of Rolo. Coffee was served. Charlotte had declined, telling her host that it would keep her up all night.

Bruce noticed how tired Charlotte was looking. It had obviously taken more out of her than he thought, having to be in the company of the friend who had betrayed her so badly. He surreptitiously looked at his watch. Fortunately, the food had taken up most of the evening and it was feasible to start the goodbyes without causing offence.

"I have to say how wonderful the evening has been Libby. Your culinary skills have impressed us all and Joshua your wines were first rate. I'm sorry to be a party pooper, but I for one will have to go home, as I have to be up early for a meeting. Thank you both for an excellent evening." The others joined in with their congratulations and praise. Charlotte had gone out into the hallway to phone for a taxi. At least there were some advantages of being sober. Just as she turned to go back into the sitting room, Libby came out to talk to her.

"Charlie, I hope we can now be friends again. Put the past behind us and move on. I'd love for you to be my Matron of Honour." Charlotte was a little taken aback. She had been Libby's Maid of Honour the first-time round. She certainly didn't want to offend her after all the trouble she had gone through that evening, but things on the friendship front were moving a little too fast for her.

"Let's discuss it over coffee, perhaps next week?" Libby nodded in approval. "I must go back in and thank Joshua. You make a lovely couple." She smiled at Libby. Libby took hold of Charlotte and hugged her.

"Thank you so much for coming. I've missed you terribly. I need your forgiveness Charlie. Let's have that coffee very soon." She let Charlotte go and Charlotte noticed tears were streaming down Libby's cheeks. Charlotte was beginning to feel guilty for abandoning her friend until she remembered why. Bruce came out just in time.

"Right then ladies, I think it's time we made a move and let the two lovebirds enjoy their celebrations in peace." Charlotte breathed a sigh of relief. Libby was getting too deep for the time of night. She mouthed a 'thank you' to Bruce who winked back at her. The taxi came quite quickly and they were off, with Joshua and Libby waving goodbye from the door. Rolo was wandering around the flowerbed watering the plants. It still seemed strange to Bruce seeing a dog in the garden where the neighbourhood children once feared to tread.

All in all, the evening was unexpectedly good. The food was excellent no one could fault it. The wine flowed in abundance so that had top marks. But when the subject of Joshua the vet came up the poor taxi driver wished he had earplugs! Everyone had something to say about him, not always polite. The general consensus was that Joshua and Libby did suit each other in a strange way. Tom couldn't help himself but he finally was able to say it out loud.

"I've never met such a pompous prick in my life." George wanted to defend Joshua, but found it hard when she agreed with her husband.

"Language please, Thomas." She was smiling at him. He knew he was in trouble and was looking forward to his punishment when they got home!

The taxi driver dropped Charlotte and Bruce off on the way to George and Tom's. They would come back the next day for their car and probably another character assassination of Joshua.

"To be fair to the vet, he has to have some good qualities

to be so besotted with Libby." Bruce was making Charlotte a hot chocolate while she checked her emails. Charlotte looked over at Bruce and thought, not for the first time, what a remarkably amiable bloke he was. He always seemed to see the good in his fellow human beings, even when it was concealed from most people's view.

"I love you, Bruce Gordon." She went over and kissed him. "Now it's bedtime and apparently you have an early meeting tomorrow. So, our Sunday lie-in will be just for me. Try not to wake me up as you leave." She was teasing him, knowing full well that that had been a ruse to leave the dinner party without it being awkward with an early departure.

"I love you, boss." He didn't like using her full name, not while it was still Whitfield. He'd have to change that as soon as he could.

CHAPTER 20

Charlotte had taken herself off to the doctor's after Bruce had gone to work on the Monday morning. Although her appointment was 10.30 a.m., she was told to come in early, with a sample, and the nurse would go through the formalities before she saw the doctor.

She was called into a side room where the nurse checked her urine and blood pressure, weight and height and explained the process of antenatal care in their practice. When the nurse had typed out all the information and results onto Charlotte's file, she was told to go back into the waiting room and the doctor would call her through presently.

She didn't have long to wait until the tannoy system called "Charlotte Whitfield to Room 3 please."

Charlotte was delighted when she walked into the room

to find a very kind looking lady doctor getting up and introducing herself.

"Hello Mrs Whitfield. I'm Doctor Toosey and I'm going to take good care of you. I have read your history, albeit briefly but I can see that you must be concerned about this pregnancy to say the least. Now it's totally understandable..." She pointed to the examination couch and gestured for Charlotte to lie on it. "So, I will just have a quick check to see if we can match dates for baby's due date, and then I can get you feeling a little more relaxed for the duration of your pregnancy." Charlotte hadn't managed to say a word. She was in awe of the way this doctor had taken charge and left her feeling that she was in capable hands. Doctor Toosey checked Charlotte's tummy and then looked at the computer screen. "Well, all looks good at the moment. Up you get and we'll work out dates." Charlotte got off the bed and straightened her clothing before walking to the doctor's desk and sitting down. She was racking her brain to remember her last period. The last one she actually remembered having had been around the time James had tried to break into the house. She got out her phone and checked her calendar to see what the date was that they had all gone to Ocean View Café.

"My last period must have been exactly twelve weeks ago." She looked up at the doctor who smiled.

"I'm so good at my job, I reckoned twelve weeks by the size of your little bundle in there." She pointed at Charlotte's tummy. "Well the next thing I must do is to get a scan organised so we can both be proved right." She picked up her phone and organised it immediately. Charlotte was impressed, but then she started over thinking. Perhaps the doctor is rushing things because she is worried. Doctor Toosey put the phone down. "Right Mrs Whitfield. If you can pop to the maternity hospital in St. Jude's Road, you know where that is? Just behind the main hospital building." Charlotte nodded. "Good. They are waiting for you now. The reason why I'm rushing it through is because I want to get you into the system as soon as possible so we can assign a midwife to you and it'll be plain sailing from there on. Any questions, any time of the day or night you can ring the number that you will get from your midwife and hopefully your mind will be put at rest. We need you to be relaxed and stress-free during this pregnancy, don't we?" Charlotte nodded.

"Thank you." Charlotte got up. For an intelligent, high-powered woman, Charlotte felt extremely vulnerable. Doctor Toosey could sense Charlotte's anxiety. She stood up too and took her hand.

"Ridiculous to tell you to stop worrying, but I'll do all I can to make sure we deliver a healthy baby for you, ok?" Charlotte smiled and nodded. The pregnancy already felt so different from the last one that it gave her hope.

On the way to the hospital's maternity department, she planned in her head how she was going to tell Bruce. She decided she'd buy a bottle of wine and cook one of his favourite meals, sausages in a large Yorkshire pudding with lashings of onion gravy. Not exactly cordon bleu and Libby would have thoroughly disapproved of the choice, but Bruce loved good old home cooking, just like his mother made. It was another endearing feature of his. Charlotte was smiling when she arrived at the reception desk.

All went well with the scan. The sonographer had turned the screen so Charlotte could see her tiny baby while all the calculations were made. The result was twelve weeks, and the sonographer handed Charlotte photos of the scan.

Charlotte left the unit in a semi-state of euphoria. She had a busy day ahead and needed to put her feet back on the ground. She popped into the wine shop opposite the office and had to think of a way of telling Bruce over the meal. She'd pick her sister's brain while she was there.

George was in the kitchen making a coffee. Charlotte looked around for Bruce but there was no sign of him. She walked up behind her sister while getting the photos out of her bag. She held them up and coughed. George turned round.

"OMG Charlie." She put the coffee jug down and grabbed the photos. Tears were running down her face. Charlotte thought George was being very emotional, could she be...? No, she mustn't even presume. Not until George tells her. But how amazing would that be? "So how far along are you?"

"The scan and the doctor agree twelve weeks." Charlotte suddenly did the maths in her head. "Oh my goodness. It was exactly three months ago I went to Scotland and Bruce and I made love for the first time. Oh George, it's so romantic. This baby has been made with love. Please let it be alright." George went over and hugged her sister.

"You'll be fine this time. We'll make sure of it. Have you told Bruce yet?"

"No. I was thinking of telling him over a dinner tonight. Any ideas how?" She checked behind her in case Bruce had come back.

"It'll have to be after the meal. What about getting him

to open a box of chocolates and putting these on the top under the lid?" She was waving the photos about.

"George, you are a genius. What a wonderful idea. I hope he'll be pleased."

"I think that'll be an understatement knowing how much Bruce loves you. Oh Charlie, I wish I could be there. Can you video it?" They laughed at the idea.

"I think it'll be a bit obvious with me holding the phone while he opens the chocolates, don't you?" Charlotte took the photos off George and put them back in her handbag. She was about to turn when a hand touched her shoulder.

"Hello, this is a nice surprise. Come to see the workers, boss?" Bruce was smiling cheekily at Charlotte. "Or have you come to take me out for lunch?"

"I'm cooking you a nice dinner so I need you to be hungry tonight. I popped in to ask you to be home early." Bruce looked baffled.

"It's not my birthday or yours. Is it an anniversary?" Charlotte looked at him and was holding herself back from just blurting the reason out.

"No, I just wanted to have a nice night in after the hectic weekend. See you later. Bye, George." She left without looking back at Bruce. She was starting to feel guilty but hoped the end result would make him see it was worth the subterfuge.

Bruce arrived back from work early. He was excited to see why Charlotte wanted him home. He now knew her too well to think it was just because she wanted a nice night in. She was up to something he could tell, but he had no idea what.

"Darling, I'm home." Bruce loved saying that every time

he walked through the front door. Charlotte thought it was sweet and looked forward to hearing it.

"I'm in the kitchen." She had opened the wine earlier and was pouring it as he walked in.

"Cheers." He took the glass from her and kissed her on the cheek as he chinked glasses. "Bit of good news for you. The Canary Wharf publishers that have been dragging their heels have finally come on board and I'm feeling a fruitful and long relationship developing." He chinked his glass with Charlotte again.

"Fantastic news, Bruce. You and George have worked hard on that account so well deserved. Dinner will be ready in about half an hour if you want to go and relax." Bruce nodded.

"I'll pop up and have a quick shower. I'm looking forward to a quiet night in. Have you checked what's on the TV?" Charlotte inwardly smiled.

"Let's treat ourselves and pay for a movie. You can check what's available when you get back down." Bruce took his wine and disappeared upstairs. Charlotte felt naughty. Leading him on about a night in watching a movie was bad, but if Bruce had checked her glass of wine he'd have guessed something was up; Ribena was a good substitute if you didn't want anyone knowing you weren't drinking red wine.

The meal was eaten and enjoyed. Charlotte had slight indigestion but she knew that she was so excited that it was self-inflicted. She needed to get Bruce into the lounge for coffee. She'd put the chocolate box on the coffee table. She put the coffee cups onto a tray and handed it to Bruce.

"Can you carry this into the lounge Bruce? I need a wee." Bruce took the tray off her and walked into the lounge. He put the coasters onto the coffee table and put the cups on them. He took the tray back into the kitchen. When he returned to the lounge Charlotte was waiting.

"I'd love a chocolate, wouldn't you? It'll just round off the meal nicely." Charlotte thought it was sounding very contrived but Bruce picked up the box and took off the lid. Charlotte waited and watched his face hoping his reaction would be favourable. He was perfectly still, staring at the box of chocolates. He looked over at Charlotte. She could see his eyes glistening in the lamplight. He looked back at the box and took out the photos. He took out a hanky from his pocket and put it to his eyes. Charlotte went over to him. He put the hanky back into his pocket and put the photos onto the coffee table. He slowly turned round and faced Charlotte. Before she could say anything, he enveloped her and took her off the ground. He showered her with kisses on her head, neck and finally passionately on her lips.

Eventually he put Charlotte down and pulled her towards the sofa.

"So, you're pleased then?" Charlotte stated the obvious but was trying to get Bruce to say something. He nodded with his lips pursed. He was trying to keep it together. He felt emotions he had never felt before. He wasn't too sure how to handle them. He buried his head into Charlotte's shoulder and just squeezed her. "You'll be pleased to know that our baby was conceived in Scotland." Bruce finally let go of her and she could see how happy he was.

"Charlotte, I love you so much. I can't even put into words how I'm feeling right now." Charlotte was beaming. She couldn't have asked for a better reaction. Bruce got up and knelt by her.

"Charlotte, will you marry me?" Charlotte looked him in the eyes.

"Bruce, I love you so much. I would love to marry you." Bruce got off his knee and pulled her to her feet.

"I want to take you upstairs and make mad passionate love to you." He cradled her and carried her up the stairs. Charlotte, for some reason, felt naughty again.

"So, I take it we won't be watching *Bridget Jones's Baby* then?" The bedroom door shut after them.

A few months later with the 'wee hoose' coming on, Bruce and Charlotte went up to Scotland to tie the knot. Their marriage was kept small and low key. Georgina was matron of honour and Tom was best man, but as Bruce and Charlotte decided on a civil ceremony they were actually just witnesses. The ceremony took place in the Registrar Offices in Forfar. Bella and Johnny had Alan to stay and the rest of the party including all Bruce's aunts, uncles and cousins stayed in Craigie Lodge. The scots knew how to organise a party so the reception Helen and Archie had arranged was wonderful. Charlotte was easily tired due to her size and so the party went on into the wee small hours without her. She was in heaven. She had the most amazing husband, and a baby growing healthily in her tummy. Her whole family and extended family were all around her. Life couldn't get any better.

Back home Bruce and George were very busy and tried to keep Charlotte away from the office. She was over half way through her pregnancy and everything was looking good. They wanted to keep it that way.

Charlotte was bored. She knew George had a meeting with an American publisher who wanted to tap into the English market and she wanted to be there. The American readers simply loved the Edwardian- and Victorian-era novels so they would be a big influence in sales for their writers.

She picked up her car keys and drove herself into town. George was getting ready for her meeting with the publisher. Charlotte checked her messages and found the woman's name, Jennifer Cosgrove.

"What time is Jennifer due?" George was happy to see her sister. She'd felt queasy all morning but thought it was the remains of a very long hangover during the wedding in Scotland.

"In about ten minutes. I need to take some paracetamol, can you watch out for her?" George rushed over the road to the chemists. By the time she got back she could see Charlotte talking to Bruce in the kitchen. As she walked in for a glass of water to take the tablets both Bruce and Charlotte were looking at her smiling. "What's going on? Why are you both looking at me like that?" Charlotte tilted her head.

"George, you know you were feeling sick the day before our wedding? Then the day we travelled home? Now you feel sick again, don't you? Have you by any chance thought of using the pregnancy test you have?" George looked shocked. How come she hadn't put two and two together? Could she be? When was her last period? She thought very quickly when the last time she needed tampons.

"O my God, the last time I was on was when you gave me that test. That was over two months ago. Why hadn't I realised? I've been so engrossed in your life that I totally overlooked my own. I need to do it now." On cue, Jennifer Cosgrove arrived.

"I'll see to her. I'm pregnant, not brain dead." Charlotte shooed her sister out and went over to start the meeting. George ran back over to the chemists and bought another test.

By the time Charlotte had finished her meeting with the American and organised another date to finalise the deal, George was back and on the telephone.

"Thank you I'll be there this evening at six o'clock, goodbye." George put her phone in her pocket and grinned at her sister. "I'm pregnant, Charlie. It's got to be at least eight weeks. I've just made an appointment with my doctor and I need to get Tom to meet me there. I'm so excited." Charlotte was too. Her dream was that George's baby and her baby would grow up together like they had. "Can you hold the fort while I get hold of Tom. I need to tell him now! Oh Charlie he's going to be so thrilled." She hugged her sister and left.

Well, thought Charlotte, it hasn't been such a boring day after all.

CHAPTER 21

~

Charlotte and Bruce had decided not to find out the sex of their baby. They wanted it to be a surprise. So, on the day Charlotte went into labour, one week after her due date, they were both beyond excited. That was until Charlotte was in full labour and with Bruce rubbing her back she wished they had never had sex, ever!

All was forgotten when a beautiful baby boy popped out, weighing a healthy 7lbs 10 ozs. Bruce cut the cord and held his son while the midwife finished off the bits Bruce needn't see. Charlotte watched father and son and thought her heart was going to burst. Baby was taken away and cleaned up while the doctor came to check on Charlotte. Bruce was sent out for a few minutes. It gave him time to phone his mum and dad and George and Alan with the news. By the time he joined Charlotte she was sitting up looking refreshed holding her son.

"What a lovely picture." Bruce took a snap on his phone. "Thank you, you clever girl, for such a bonnie bairn." He leant over and kissed her.

"He definitely looks like an Alexander, don't you think?" Bruce smiled. It was the name he was hoping she'd choose, but didn't want to influence her. They had a short list of boys and girls names.

"Alexander is a very fine name. Hello Alexander. Welcome to the world. Happy birthday." He kissed the baby on the head. Alexander opened his eyes. Both parents were staring at him in wonder.

"Off you go Daddy, find yourself something useful to do for a while. We have to feed baby. Now dear, let's give it a go." Bruce took off before the midwife got her tits out. He had to laugh. What was it about medical personnel that insist on using the royal 'we'? Charlotte will be feeding the baby, not the midwife.

Charlotte and Alexander were allowed home the next day. Feeding had got into a pattern after a lot of encouragement from the midwife. Bruce spent most of his time just watching his wife and son. His job was to keep visitors at a minimum, except family, of course. Alan decided he would be Pops to Alexander. He thought Granddad made him sound too old. George was a godsend helping Charlotte with the embarrassing bits that men shouldn't even know about. She was also good with Alexander helping with the winding and changing. She said she wanted to do it for the practice.

"It'll be slightly different for you George, with a baby girl." George and Tom had wanted to know what colour to paint the nursery; or that was their excuse finding out the sex of their baby.

"I can't wait for her to be here. They are going to have so much fun growing up together. Alexander Gordon and India Harvey, will the world be ready for the two of them?" The girls laughed. "I wish Mummy was here to see us." George missed her mother more and more as her pregnancy progressed. Questions she had to ask her midwife she would have rather asked her mother. Charlotte had felt the same. Somehow, she knew her mother was watching over them both.

A few weeks after Charlotte had brought Alexander home she asked Bruce to put the baby in the car and take her to the hospital. Bruce looked concerned.

"There's nothing wrong. I just want you and Alexander to humour me. No questions, but all will be revealed." Bruce put Alexander in his car seat and went out to the car. Charlotte went up to her room and opened the top of her wardrobe. She took out a box with a folder in. Out of the folder she took an envelope. She carefully put it in her pocket and went out to the car.

They pulled up in the hospital carpark and Bruce took Alexander out of the car. Charlotte linked arms with Bruce and told him they were going to a garden behind the main wing.

As they rounded the corner Charlotte still got the loveliest feeling seeing all the teddies and balloons making the garden look alive with warmth and happiness, despite what was really under the flowers and plants.

She took Bruce over to a bench and he put Alexander's

seat on it and sat next to him. Charlotte sat by Bruce and took out the envelope.

"I want you to look at this photograph." Bruce took it from Charlotte. "It is Faith, my little daughter. I wanted you and Alexander to come and meet her." She got up and walked towards a small stone pillow with a perfectly carved stone baby lying asleep on it. Bruce walked over to it and looked at the plaque.

"Faith Peters, playing with the angels." He turned to Charlotte and realised that the baby she had miscarried was the baby in the photograph and was buried in that garden. "Oh Charlotte, come here." He pulled her towards him and hugged her. "Why didn't you tell me? You shouldn't have kept this to yourself." He could feel her body shaking slightly and knew she was crying. He held her until she had stopped.

"The paramedics found her when they were examining me and took her to the hospital with me. It wasn't until I had regained consciousness that I even knew they had found her. The nurse brought her in and let me hold her and say a proper goodbye." Bruce looked at the photograph again. The baby was so small.

"Faith." He went down onto his knees and looked at the baby on the stone pillow. "Well Faith, meet your baby brother Alexander." He turned and pointed at the car seat where Alexander was sleeping. "When he's older we will let him know what a beautiful sister he had. Good night little Faith, sleep tight." He blew her a kiss and got up. He placed the photograph back into the envelope he took from Charlotte and put it back in her bag. "Keep it safe until her brother is old enough to understand." He picked up the car seat and took Charlotte's hand. "Come on Mrs Gordon, let's go home. We'll come back soon little Faith." He said over his shoulder. "I'll take care of your mummy and brother for you, I promise." Charlotte was glad she had shared her secret with Bruce. Bruce felt honoured that she had shared something so personal and private with him.

Charlotte had not heard from Libby since the dinner party, all those months ago. She had actually surprised herself by being a little worried. The coffee they were going to have the next week never happened. After the baby news and Bruce's proposal, and then all the arrangements for their own wedding, Charlotte had put Libby to the back of her mind. It was harsh, but she felt she needed to enjoy her good news without the old bad news coming back to haunt her.

She wondered if she was married, or even still with her vet, Joshua. Bruce had gone back to work and she was at home with Alexander, with plenty of time on her hands. She decided to ring her and let her know about the baby.

"Hello, Elizabeth Fisher-White. How can I help you?" Charlotte was shocked, to say the least. Libby must have married, and she got a double-barrelled name back after all.

"Hello Libby, it's Charlotte. How are you?" Charlotte waited for an answer.

"Oh, hello Charlotte. It's nice to hear from you. I'm fine thank you and yourself?"

Since when did Libby start calling Charlie, Charlotte? Of course, Joshua didn't believe in shortening names.

"I wanted to let you know that I have a little baby boy called Alexander." She waited again and began to think Libby was being rude.

"How lovely for you. Joshua and I are far too busy to have children yet. He has set up a private practice here in our house. It's full-on, but such fun. I have been training as a veterinary nurse but I have to admit it's not going well. I'd rather be in the kitchen creating than clipping dog claws." She laughed. *"So, I hear you and Bruce got married too. We decided to keep it simple and popped over to the Caribbean for a few weeks and got married on the beach with a couple of American tourists as our witnesses. It was great fun."* Something in the tone of Libby's voice made Charlotte think it wasn't as much fun as she was making out; poor old Libby. She suspected it was all Joshua's idea.

"Well when you have a free moment please pop over for a coffee and you can meet Alexander. It's been lovely talking to you Libby, but I can hear him stirring and that will mean feeding time. Take care and as I say pop over anytime." Charlotte heard Libby take a deep breath.

"Thank you, Charlie, I will. It's been so good to hear from you. Hope to see you soon. Lots of love to you and Bruce. Goodbye." There was a definite sniff as she said goodbye. She'd reverted to calling her Charlie too. Charlotte was sure she was crying. Poor Libby, she was really glad she had made contact with her again. It sounded like she needed a friend and Charlotte was ready to be that again.

Five months after Alexander was born Georgina and Tom had their beautiful baby girl, India. She was perfect in every way. Charlotte joked that they would have a crèche added to the office so they could both work. Tom and Bruce had other ideas. A compromise was agreed. A childminder would look after the babies during the day at Charlotte's house and both girls could work from there with the occasional visit to the office.

One morning, Bruce had said goodbye to Charlotte and Alexander and had driven off to work. Charlotte had given Alexander his cereal and left him munching on a rusk while she tidied away the breakfast things. She heard the letterbox bang and went to look at the post. There was a letter addressed to her with a Devon postmark. She was intrigued. She was sure she didn't know anyone from Devon. She sat down with a fresh cup of coffee and opened it. It was from James.

Dear Charlie

I hope you are well and happy.

I've been trying to write this letter for a long time now, but needed to get my head in the right place. My medication has worked remarkably well and I'm thinking clearer than I have in a long time.

I wanted to tell you that I can't forgive myself for the way I've treated you. I am so sorry for all the misery I have put you through. Even though I now have been told that it wasn't my fault, it doesn't make me feel any better.

I have only a vague recollection of the day I forced you to that house. You must have been terrified but hopefully you knew that I could never physically hurt you.

I hope eventually you can forgive me and accept my apology. My therapist told me it would help us both move on. He's quite a decent chap actually.

You'll be pleased to know that I am teaching some of the residents here computer skills to help them when they are released. I'm also catching up on advanced computer programming for when I can resume my life outside these walls. So life for me is looking up for the first time in months. I will have to take medication long term, but it's a small price to pay for the ability to function like a normal human being again.

Please send my best regards to Bruce. I will be writing to him to apologise too. Something tells me that it's all worked out for the good for you two though! I'm glad. You both deserve to be happy.

All the best
James

As Charlotte folded it back into the envelope, she mused that her nightmare had started with the postman's delivery of a letter, how ironic that it had ended with one too.

THE END

ND - #0154 - 270225 - C0 - 203/127/15 - PB - 9781861518361 - Gloss Lamination